Getting
REVENGE
on Lauren Wood

Also by Eileen Cook

What Would Emma Do?

The Education of Hailey Kendrick

Getting REVENGE on Lauren Wood

EILEEN COOK

SIMON PULSE

New York   London   Toronto   Sydney

SIMON PULSE

An imprint of Simon & Schuster Children's Publishing Division

1230 Avenue of the Americas, New York, NY 10020

First Simon Pulse paperback edition December 2010

Copyright © 2010 by Eileen Cook

All rights reserved, including the right of reproduction in whole or in part in any form.

SIMON PULSE and colophon are registered trademarks of Simon & Schuster, Inc.

Also available in a Pulse hardcover edition.

For information about special discounts for bulk purchases, please contact Simon & Schuster Special Sales at 1-866-506-1949 or business@simonandschuster.com.

The Simon & Schuster Speakers Bureau can bring authors to your live event. For more information or to book an event contact the Simon & Schuster Speakers Bureau at 1-866-248-3049 or visit our website at www.simonspeakers.com.

Designed by Paul Weil

The text of this book was set in Adobe Garamond.

Manufactured in the United States of America

2 4 6 8 10 9 7 5 3 1

Library of Congress Control Number 2009938355

ISBN 978-1-4169-7433-8 (hc)

ISBN 978-1-4424-0976-7 (pbk)

ISBN 978-1-4169-8537-2 (eBook)

Chapter One

Last night I dreamed I dissected Lauren Wood in Earth Sciences class. She was wearing her blue and white cheerleader outfit, the pleated skirt fanned out and the sweater cut right down the middle. She lay there, unmoving, staring straight up at the ceiling tiles. She was annoyed. I could tell from the way her jaw thrust forward and her lips pressed together in a thin line. I opened up her chest, peeling her ribs back like a half-opened Christmas present, and the entire class leaned in to get a good look.

"As I suspected," I declared, "no heart." I pointed with my scalpel to the chest cavity, where nothing but a black lump of coal squatted in the lipstick-red center. The class leaned back with a sigh, equally appalled and fascinated. The mysterious inner workings of Lauren Wood exposed for all to see.

"Earth to Helen."

My Earth Sciences teacher, Mr. Porto, was staring at me,

waiting for an answer. Someone behind me snickered. I hadn't heard the question. I had been reliving my dream from last night and must have spaced out. I looked at my desk in case the answer was there, but the only thing on my page was a doodle of an anatomically correct heart. I didn't think Mr. Porto would be impressed with my artwork at this particular moment. I prayed for time to speed up and make the bell ring, but the clock kept on ticking one second at a time.

"People, I know vacation begins in a few days, but at the moment you still need to worry more about your final exam than about your summer plans. Can anyone else list for me the six kingdoms of the scientific classification system?" Mr. Porto asked.

He looked around the room for a victim. I slouched down in my seat and attempted to resume my train of thought and natural state of invisibility.

Before the incident there hadn't been a single moment of my life without Lauren in it. We were born in the same hospital, her the day before me. They placed us side by side in the nursery, our first sleepover. Helen Worthington right next to Lauren Wood. Even alphabetically, Lauren came before me. Lauren was in every one of my birthday photos—from age one, when she has her fist buried in my cake, to fourteen when we are both posing supermodel style for the camera, Lauren's outstretched arm covering part of my face. Looking back, I can see how she always had to be front and center.

Speaking of needing to be front and center, Carrie Edwards

must have been running for star biology student. She waved her arm like she was flagging down traffic until Mr. Porto called on her.

"Eubacteria, arche bacteria, protists, fungi, plants, and animals," Carrie spouted off. She paused as if she expected applause. I drew a cartoon of a cheerleader on my paper. I gave her a giant mouth. My eyes slid back to the clock and watched it tick over the final seconds. The bell rang out, and everyone stood up together and jostled toward the door.

"Be sure to look over chapter twenty-two before the exam! I don't want to hear anyone saying they didn't know they were supposed to know the material. Consider this your last warning," Mr. Porto yelled to everyone's back. The volume in the hallway seemed even louder than usual. Everyone was excited to see the year come to an end. Next year we would be seniors, on top of the world. I slipped through the hallway by myself. A few people nodded in my direction, but nobody said anything to me.

It had been the end of the school year when it happened three years ago, only a few days after my fourteenth birthday. Sometimes I look at the photo from the party to see if I can find any clues. Lauren and I are both smiling. My smile is easy to explain— I didn't know what was coming—but Lauren would have known. She had already put pieces of her plan into action, but there isn't a sign of regret on her face. No hesitation at all, just her wide smile. I suppose she expected me to be grateful that she let me have my birthday before she brought the world crashing down around me. It was the least she could do. After all, what are friends for?

Chapter Two

THREE YEARS AGO—SPRING, EIGHTH GRADE

I never should have worn my jean skirt. I wasn't fat, but I was definitely pushing the chubby border. I wanted to wear the skirt because I thought it looked good, but I quickly regretted it. It was too warm for tights, and my bare thighs had been rubbing together as I walked, and they felt like they were going to blister. I shifted again on the bleacher, trying to give my legs their own breathing space.

"What's the matter with you?" Lauren asked. "Stop moving around."

"I'm hot."

"I know I am, but what are you?" she said with a smirk and a raised eyebrow.

"Ha. Lauren Wood, stand-up comic extraordinaire."

Lauren took a regal bow. It was good to see her joking around again, even if it was a lame joke. The idea of starting high school seemed to freak her out more than me. For the past few weeks she'd been in a rotten mood, and everything set her off. That week alone we'd had at least four fights, one where she didn't speak to me for a full day because she thought I was making fun of what she had brought for lunch. Lauren was a huge fan of the silent treatment when she was ticked at you. I would end up begging her to forgive me, even when I was pretty sure I hadn't done anything wrong. It had been established years ago that Lauren was the drama queen and I was the diplomat. I had pleaded with her to stop being mad about the lunch fight. I even declared I was sincerely sorry if her Oreos had suffered any emotional distress on my account. I didn't care about sacrificing my pride. Keeping my best friend happy was worth it.

"Do you see that guy over there?" Lauren yanked her head to the left. I leaned forward to look, but she rammed her bony elbow into my side.

"Don't look at him."

"How am I supposed to see him if I don't look at him?"

"I mean look, but don't *look* like you're looking. God."

I leaned forward casually and then let my eyes drift over the crowd. The gym was packed. Lincoln High was huge, with at least seven hundred students in every grade. Students came from different middle schools all across the city. Each spring the school did a welcome event for the incoming freshmen so that we could bond as a class. We had already been given a tour of the school, taken to an extracurricular "fair" so we could see all the clubs and teams we had to choose from, and subjected to a hot lunch from the cafeteria. Now we were rounding out the day with a rah-rah school spirit rally. All of this was supposed to help keep us from freaking out next fall, as if not knowing how to find our way to our lockers was the problem. If schools really wanted to reduce the anxiety level, they would distribute student handbooks with useful information like which bathroom belongs to the stoner kids, and how the sink in the biology lab always sprays water, and how under no circumstances should you order the hot lunch on the day they serve "shepherd's pie" because it's leftovers from last week with boxed mashed potatoes on top. They never tell you the useful stuff. That you have to figure out on your own.

Lauren was taking the whole thing very seriously. She scribbled down notes during the fair, grabbed handouts from each table, and ranked activities in preference from best to worse. I suspected that later her mom would help her turn it into a spreadsheet complete with social acceptability ratings.

My eyes scanned the rows of people. At first I couldn't figure out who had caught Lauren's eye, but then I saw him. Lauren usually went for the Mr. All-American type, blond, fresh off the country club look. This guy was different. He was leaning back, his elbows on the bleacher seat behind him. He was wearing what looked like a vintage T-shirt. Not some shirt from Old Navy that was meant to *look* like a cool vintage shirt, but really wasn't—his was the real thing, pale and soft from years of washing. He had red hair that was cut short in the back, but a little longer in the front. I was staring at him when he looked over and met my eyes. He gave a smile and then a small salute in my direction.

"Oh my God, he saw me." I yanked my head back and Lauren leaned forward to see the situation for herself.

"He's waving," she whispered. She looked at me and we burst out laughing. "Is he looking at me?" Lauren asked.

"I'm not looking again. You look."

"No way. You look."

I leaned forward again and risked a quick glance. He was staring over. He gave another wave. I found myself smiling and then figured what the hell, and waved back. Lauren grabbed my arm, practically snapping it off at the elbow, and yanked it back down. I leaned back so fast I nearly fell off the bench, my legs kicking out.

"What are you doing?" Lauren asked. She looked around to see if anyone had noticed that she was stuck sitting next to me, the dork.

"Well, it's not like he doesn't know we were checking him out. We can't act casual now."

"Oh God, he's coming over here. Do I look okay?" Lauren gave her teeth a quick wipe with a finger in case there was any hot lunch caught in there. I looked her up and down. She looked the way she always looked to me.

"Hey." The good-looking waver guy stood at the end of our row, his hands in his pockets. He smiled and I felt my stomach turn over slowly, but in a good way, not in a hot-lunch-gone-bad kind of way. Lauren giggled but didn't say anything.

"Hey," I answered back as it seemed one of us should say something.

"I'm Tyler."

"Helen, and this is my best friend, Lauren," I said, and Lauren gave another giggle. She was doing this thing with her eyes like she had something in them; they were fluttering up and down spastically. It must have had a hypnotizing effect because Tyler was staring at her with a sort of vacant smile on his face. With everyone identified we seemed to have run out of things to talk about. I looked down at his T-shirt and felt myself break into a smile. It was the logo for the Sundance Film Festival.

"Movie fan?" I asked.

"Yeah, you?" he asked, breaking eye contact with Lauren.

"Uh-huh. I love old movies best, all the *Bringing Up Baby* or *The Philadelphia Story* stuff."

"I'm into more current stuff. Sort of edgy. The Coen brothers . . . stuff like that."

"Curtiz was better," I countered.

"Who?" he asked.

This guy thought he was into film and he didn't know Curtiz? Puh-leeze.

"Director of *Casablanca*," I answered.

"*Casablanca*? Could you pick something more out of date?"

Lauren interrupted. We both looked over at her. She gave her hair a toss.

Tyler laughed as if she had said something profoundly amusing.

"So what kind of movies do you like?" Tyler asked Lauren.

"Romances," she said, doing the fluttery eye thing again.

"How can you say you're a film nut if you don't like *Casablanca*? That's like saying you love ice cream except for vanilla."

Both of them looked at me, but neither spoke. It seemed like everyone had agreed to act like I hadn't said anything at all.

"Nice to meet you, Lauren." Tyler smiled at her and then looked at me blankly.

"Helen," I reminded him. "Nice to meet you too." I felt my face flush. Someone at the front of the gym was testing the microphone, calling out for people to take their seats.

"I should go." Tyler leaned over and took my pencil from my hand. "Here's my number. Why don't you guys give me a call if you want to catch a movie sometime." He scribbled his number on the top of my sheet. I looked at it like I had never seen a phone number before. I certainly had never seen one that a boy had given me. I might have to frame it.

"Yeah, okay," I mumbled, my face turning bright red.

"We'll see you around," Lauren added, and he gave her a nod before heading back to his friends. I watched him walk away. I turned around to see if Lauren noticed how nicely his jeans fit, and she was staring at me with her lips tight and thin. Uh-oh.

"God, Helen, why don't you throw yourself at him?"

"What?"

"You knew I liked him, but you practically attacked him when he came over."

"You like him?"

Lauren cocked her head to the side and then looked away. "Whatever."

"I was just talking to him."

"You like movies? Why, I *love* movies. Let me bore you with all the stuff I know about stupid old movies," Lauren said in a high squeaky voice.

"Sorry." I tried to think of where I went wrong. I could tell she was annoyed with me, but it wasn't like I brought up movies out of nowhere.

"Just forget it." Lauren crossed her arms and stared out at the gym floor. "You have to cut that out."

"Cut what out?"

"Acting like a total dork all the time. We're going to be in high school, so it wouldn't kill you to act normal once in a while. I mean, it's one thing to like all that weird stuff, but you don't have to brag about it any time we meet someone."

"Old movies aren't weird. It's not like I like taxidermy or something."

Lauren sighed. "Talking about taxidermy is weird too. It's like you don't even know what normal is." We sat there not talking until the band began playing the Lincoln school song and the assembly officially started. I risked glancing over at Tyler one more time. He was staring in our direction, and I turned away quickly as if I had been caught doing something wrong. I don't know why I bothered. He was looking in our direction, but the only person he saw was Lauren. People always liked Lauren. I was the bonus item, what people got for free when they hung out with her.

The assembly went on forever. If one more person got up to tell us how many opportunities awaited us during the next four years I was going to stick a sharpened pencil in my ear.

"I have to go to the bathroom," I whispered to Lauren.

"Thanks for the update."

"Seriously, I have to go. Come with me."

"Not now." Lauren pointed toward the stage. Lincoln's cheerleading squad was doing a routine. "We should try out in the fall." She rummaged through the stack of handouts for the one that gave the details on the cheer squad.

I looked at Lauren as if she had announced that she wanted to take up cattle roping. We weren't exactly cheerleader material. Cheerleaders do not have thighs that rub together, and Lauren, who didn't have the same thigh issues, suffered from near terminal clumsiness. She couldn't do a cartwheel without falling over.

"Are you kidding?"

"What? We could be cheerleaders."

"Have you ever noticed that the cheerleaders are the most popular girls in school?"

"Yeah."

"We're not the most popular girls." I hated to be the one to point this out to her, but you'd think she would have noticed by now.

"My mom says high school is completely different. It's like a fresh start."

I rolled my eyes. Fresh start, maybe. Complete life do-over? I don't think so.

Lauren went back to watching them intently, as if her life depended on memorizing the dance routine. I slipped past her, leaving her to her cheerleading daydreams.

The bathrooms under the bleachers doubled as the girls' locker room. The room smelled like a mix of chlorine, mildewed towels, and Secret deodorant. I pushed a stall door open and sat down. As soon as I was seated the stall door started to creep back open. I kicked it shut and it flew right past the latch and swung out into the bathroom. Great, one broken latch and now I was on display for the entire locker room. This was exactly the kind of thing that schools should give you a warning on but don't.

Suddenly I heard someone laugh. I finished as fast as I could and yanked my skirt back down, trying to look casual. I waited there for a moment, but no one came into the bathroom. I took a few steps toward the sinks, and the voices and laughter got louder. There was a door leading to the pool, bolted from the locker room side. I pressed my ear against the door. The voices were coming from there for certain.

I slipped the bolt open, the click sounding very loud in the empty bathroom, but the voices on the other side didn't change. They hadn't heard anything. I pulled the door open slowly and peered through the crack.

Holy. Shit.

There were soap bubbles everywhere; bubbles spreading like a foamy blob across the tile floor. The swimming pool was covered in a frothy concoction, like a giant latte. At the back of the room near the diving board a group of seniors stood pouring bottles of lemon yellow dish soap into the water. They were laughing, and Matt Ryan, who I knew from the local paper as the school's star athlete, was standing back trying to capture the whole thing on his camera phone. He was the one who saw me. He winked at me then pressed his finger to his mouth, in the universal symbol for *shhh*, and I knew I should pretend I never saw a thing. I shut the door quietly and slid the bolt closed.

"What are you doing?"

I jumped and whirled around to face Lauren.

"There are a bunch of seniors dumping soap into the pool."

"Get out!" Lauren walked past me and slid the bolt back on the door.

"I don't think we're supposed to know about it."

"Duh." Lauren pulled the door open and peered through the crack. She gave a tiny squeal and shut the door. "It must be the senior prank."

Senior prank was a long-standing Lincoln High tradition.

Each class tried to come up with a way to outdo the class before. I figured by the time we were seniors we would have to come up with something worthy of making CNN, like kidnapping the prime minister of Canada.

"They must have dumped at least a dozen bottles of soap into the pool," I said.

"We should go. The assembly is almost over, and we don't want to be caught down here." Lauren took off. Once we were in the hall I looked behind me. There was a wall of bubbles pressing against the frosted glass window in the door that led directly to the pool. I jogged after Lauren.

The whole thing seemed funny. It was a prank after all, a joke. Just good clean soapy fun. I thought I was pretty cool to be in on it, especially considering I wasn't even officially a freshman yet.

The school administration took a dimmer view of the situation. Apparently dish soap and pool filters are a bad combination. Then there was the fact that one of the school janitors slipped on the soapy pool deck and fell, pulling his knee all out of whack. Rumor had it he was suing the school in some kind of worker's compensation case for millions of dollars, but that part might not have been true. What was a fact was that the school administration was on a mission to find out who was behind the whole thing.

The day after my birthday party an article appeared in the Sunday paper saying the seniors responsible had been caught.

The paper showed a photo of Principal LaPoint looking stern with his arms crossed over his chest. He was quoted as calling those caught the "ringleaders," like it was a major crime versus a senior prank. He was forbidding those four students from attending either prom or graduation. He wanted to withhold their diplomas altogether, but apparently the school board wasn't willing to go that far. There were quotes in the paper from people around town, most of whom thought the punishment was too severe, although there were a few who seemed to think the death penalty might be in order.

The first hint I had that anything was wrong, that the story would involve me at all, was on Monday morning. I was wearing a new soft white short sleeve sweater that I had gotten for my birthday. I was in a good mood until I got to my locker. SNITCH was written in black marker across the door. It was underlined three times. I walked up slowly, my finger extended. The ink looked still wet, but it was dry. It didn't smudge. I heard someone laugh and turned around to see a group of girls looking over from across the hall before they scurried away, still laughing. As I walked to math class I noticed it—everyone was staying far away from me. An invisible force field between me and the rest of the world. No one got closer than a few feet. It was like I had developed leprosy over the weekend.

I was walking into the classroom when someone bumped hard into my back. My book and papers went flying to the floor. I whirled around and Bill from my math class stood there looking at me.

"What?" he asked, his voice flat. I could hear his friends laughing.

I bent down to pick up my stuff. No one said anything to me in math. I hadn't been the social butterfly before, but this was different. I felt people staring at me, but when I looked around, no one would meet my eyes. My stomach felt hot and tight, and I wanted to throw up. Even Mr. Grady, our teacher, seemed annoyed with me. The whole morning was like that. I kept trying to find Lauren, but she wasn't in English or at her locker between classes. When I saw her standing in the lunch line getting her food I had never been so glad to see anyone in my whole life. I had to fight the urge to run over to her.

"Where have you been?" I asked.

Lauren looked at me like she had never seen me before. It was like I was stuck in a weird sci-fi movie.

"What do you want?" she asked holding her tray between us like a barrier.

"What's with you? I need to talk to you." I touched her elbow. Lauren yanked away and her tray lurched, slopping orange red ravioli sauce onto my new sweater. We both looked down at the spreading stain. Everyone else in the cafeteria was gaping at us.

"Don't touch me."

"Lauren? Why are you mad at me? Why is everybody mad at me?"

Someone standing in line gave a disbelieving snort.

"I didn't think you would ever do something like that," she said.

"Like what?"

"Tell on the seniors. I mean, it isn't just you; by telling, you make our whole class look like a bunch of losers. We all have to fit in at Lincoln High next year, and now we're going to be known as part of the class that ratted out the most popular seniors. Everyone will connect us with what you did. It was just a prank, Helen." Lauren's voice was so loud I was pretty sure everyone in the cafeteria could hear her.

"But I didn't tell," I said softly.

"There's no point lying about it now. Everyone already knows."

I felt a hot rush of tears in my throat choking off what I was going to say. I walked stiffly out of the cafeteria as kids yelled things after me. I didn't even stop by my locker; I walked straight out of the school and went home. I peeled off my ruined sweater, stuffed it under the bed, and crawled in. When my mom came home I told her I was sick.

I stayed home sick for the entire week. It wasn't even lying. I felt awful. I didn't want to eat anything and even though I was tired, I couldn't sleep. On Friday I went over to Lauren's house. I had to find a way to make things right. I could live with everyone else being mad, but I couldn't stand to be on the outs with my best friend. Lauren was in the backyard with a guy I didn't recognize. They were both wearing sweats. I stood at the gate and watched. He was spotting her, helping her learn how to do a cartwheel.

"Keep your legs up, nice and straight."

"I'm trying."

"You can do it. It's just a confidence thing. You think you'll fall, so you do. Just believe, and then up and over."

Lauren turned a perfect cartwheel. She gave a squeal and jumped into his arms. That's when she saw me.

"Helen."

We stood awkwardly looking at each other.

"This is Mark, my gymnastics instructor. My mom hired him."

Mark made his excuses and left.

"Still thinking of trying out for cheerleading, huh?"

"Mmm-hmm."

"I didn't tell anyone, Lauren. You have to believe me." The words came rushing out in one breath. My eyes burned and threatened to spill over. Lauren crossed her arms and sighed.

"Don't start crying again," she said, her voice sounding tired.

"Someone else must have told on them, or maybe one of them got cold feet and ratted out the others. Maybe together we can figure out who did it." Lauren loved mysteries. I was hoping to convince her that this would be a fun one to solve.

"God, just give it up. No one else told."

I looked at her and felt my stomach ice over. I felt things fall into place.

"You . . ." My voice trailed off.

"Me."

"Why?"

"Do you remember when Principal LaPoint talked about how many opportunities we'll have in the next few years?"

I nodded.

"I'm taking one of them."

"What are you talking about?"

"Did you know Emily Watson called me?"

"Who?"

"Emily Watson. She's a junior. She'll be a senior next year. She's captain of the cheerleading squad. She was very appreciative that I was willing to tell who ratted out her friends. When I told her how I was scared that I wouldn't have any friends since you were my best friend, she told me that I don't have to worry. She'll make sure I meet lots of people next year."

"I didn't rat out anyone. You did."

"Yeah, but that wasn't a problem. The truth isn't important. What matters is what people *think* is the truth. If I'm going to be somebody, then I need people on my side." She looked over at me. "People who are in a position to get me what I want."

I sat down hard on the ground, the air whooshing out me.

"But why?"

"There isn't always a big reason why. It just is."

"But you're my best friend."

"And you're happy with good enough. You don't care about dressing the right way or being invited to the right parties. You're happy to rent movies on a Friday night. Not even new movies. You want to rent stuff no one has seen in like a hundred years. I want to go out. I want to be invited out. We were always second string, but now I have a chance to make the A-list."

"And that matters so much?"

"Of course it matters." Lauren tossed her hands in the air and paced back and forth. "My mom tells me that the friends you have in high school determine who your friends are in college, and then who your friends are for the rest of your life."

"Well, my mom says you can't buy friendship," I countered.

"And your mom is a hippie who doesn't even use deodorant."

"She does too. It's just that rock crystal kind."

"Whatever."

"So you're just done with me? That's it?" I could hear my voice getting tight and high. This wasn't going the way I had planned. I had figured my problem would be convincing her I hadn't told. I wasn't prepared for this conversation at all.

Lauren sat down next to me and pulled a few strands of grass out of the lawn. We sat there quietly for a minute. "Nothing is forever, you know. Once I'm popular, we can be friends again and then you'll be popular too. It will all be worth it."

"What makes you think I'll want to be your friend?"

"What makes you think you'll have other options?"

Chapter Three

The last two weeks of eighth grade were vile. Someone mashed spoiled tuna fish through the vents in my locker so that everything I owned stunk. A person in my English class smeared glue on my chair. No one talked to me, but everyone was whispering about me behind my back. People left mean notes in my books, and the janitor stopped even bothering to clean my locker door, since every time he did, someone else would write *SNITCH* across it. I stopped eating lunch in the cafeteria after someone spit on my food tray. For those last two weeks of school I sat in the back of the library during lunch and pretended to study. During gym class someone dumped my clothes on the wet shower floor, so I had to wear my gym uniform for the rest of the day. I cried every night. My parents talked to the school administrators, who said there was nothing they could do. I would have to "ride it out."

My mom tried to convince me that it would be better next year and I would make new friends, but I wasn't buying it. The way I figured it, high school would be worse. Instead of having one hundred fifty classmates trying to make me miserable, I would have seven hundred. Unless you counted the other grades, in which case I would have thousands of people dedicated to making my life hell. I was certain that my reputation as a ratfink had spread to every school across town.

My parents are huge believers in karma. Actually, they're huge believers in a bunch of stuff: chi, feng shui, the benefits of being vegan, the superiority of natural fabrics. They believe in everything from Buddha to fairies. Most of the time I shrug off what they say. They kept telling me that somehow things would just magically work out and the universe would take care of things. I was preparing for the idea that I may have to run away from home, when it turned out my parents were right. My dad was offered a job in New York. Thank god for karma.

Technically it wasn't New York City, it was some town just outside the city, but it was still good enough for me. Heck, I would have gone anywhere, including remote Alaska. I just wanted to be as far away from Terrace, Michigan, as possible. We were moving. I was so happy, I didn't even mind doing the packing. For once the universe seemed to have noticed what I needed.

From the time school ended until we moved at the end of July, I didn't hear from Lauren once. I guess she was too busy focusing on mastering the intricacies of the perfect cartwheel to find time to say good-bye to her best friend. She might have forgotten all about me, but I certainly never forgot about her. Not for one single day.

Chapter Four

$\mathscr{I}$'d be lying if I didn't admit that over the next three years, even from New York, I thought about getting back at Lauren somehow. But it was never anything specific. Once I dressed up a Barbie doll in a cheerleader outfit and tossed it into the giant wood chipper in the park. I grinned as the flesh-colored plastic sprayed out in tiny half-moon crescents onto the ground. Although I thought about it all the time, I didn't think I would ever really do anything about the situation. Logistics alone would make it impossible. I lived halfway across the country from her. Revenge by mail didn't seem that satisfying. Not to mention there are laws against sending anthrax. I hoped my parents were right, that karma would balance things out and Lauren would have some (or preferably all) of the following things happen to her:

1. She would be permanently disfigured by a virulent acne condition.

2. She would suffer some type of cheerleading accident involving choking to death on a wayward pom-pom.
3. Her hair would fall out due to a shampoo manufacturer's defect.
4. All the lies she told would come back to haunt her by turning her tongue black.

But none of these things happened. I watched her from a distance by stalking her Facebook page. I told myself I didn't care, but I couldn't stop checking to see what she was doing. I kept waiting for something to go wrong for her, but nothing did. For the next three years she went from one success to another. She mastered the cartwheel the summer before freshman year and made the cheerleading squad. She started dating Justin Ryan, the younger brother of the popular Matt Ryan of soap bubble fame. Justin, like his brother before him, was the star of every team at Lincoln High and looked like an Abercrombie & Fitch ad. Lauren was always posting pictures of the two of them, arms wrapped around each other. She was active with the drama club and a shoo-in to get the lead for senior year. She was always getting tagged in smiling groups mugging for the camera. She would be right in the middle, her giant, white horse teeth reflecting the camera flash. Her friends were always posting notes on her page about how she was their "BFF!!" and how her "party last night rocked!" Her friends used exclamation points for everything. She was at the top of the social ladder at Lincoln High.

It wasn't like I didn't have my own life. Things weren't bad or anything. I loved New York. I wasn't popular in my new school, but I wasn't unpopular either. To be honest, I was one of those people that no one noticed. When I first moved I didn't want to make friends with anyone. I felt like my whole life was one exposed nerve, and I couldn't stand to have anyone close enough to touch me. By the time I wanted to make friends, everyone else had moved on. I already had the reputation of being a loner. I wore a lot of black but didn't quite go far enough to be Goth. I didn't play sports or an instrument. I liked art, but drawing isn't exactly a group activity. I didn't really put an effort into changing things. Once you've been classified into a certain role, it's hard to make a change. Or maybe it just seemed easier to be by myself. I was friendly with a lot of people, but I didn't have any true friends. Sometimes it sucked that there wasn't anyone to talk to about things, but on the bright side, no one was close enough to screw me over either.

The only picture of me in this year's yearbook was my standard school photo. No clubs, no sports teams, no student government. No shot of me surrounded by friends. In fact, it would be easy to forget I existed at all.

Three years after she stabbed me in the back, Lauren was the queen of Lincoln High, and the fact that she lied and destroyed my life to be popular didn't seem to matter to anyone except me.

Sometimes karma does a shitty job of evening the score.

Chapter Five

I was lying on my bed reading my history homework. We were studying the French Revolution, and I was doodling Lauren's giant teeth on the picture of Marie Antoinette being led to the guillotine. I sat up when my dad tapped on the door. He and my mom stood in the doorway.

"Hey, poppet," Dad said, scratching his arm. My parents' latest thing was clothing made from hemp. It was supposed to be super-renewable and great for the planet, but my dad was having some kind of allergic reaction to the whole thing. He kept breaking out in these red hives, but he continued to wear it. Saving the planet wasn't supposed to be easy.

Dad looked at what I was reading and broke out a big smile. "Ah *liberté, egalité, fraternité*." He took the book from my hand and flipped through the pages. He had majored in French in college, one of those degrees that might have been useful if, for example, we lived in France. My mom took a step forward so she was standing right next to him. She tucked her hair behind an ear. It was so curly that it instantly sprung back out.

"What's up?" I asked.

"We have some good news." Dad rubbed his hands on his pant legs and my mom gave him a reassuring nod. "The school has approved my research grant."

"Dad, that's awesome!" The alternative school where my dad taught was always out of money, so for them to support anything was a big deal. Also, research wasn't completely their thing. It was more of a live-and-let-live kind of place. His eyes shifted over to my mom.

"Your dad will have a chance to look into the role of meditation in healing. He might even have time to write the book he's always talked about."

"Okay." I drew the word out slowly so that it was more of a question. My dad has talked about writing a book on alternative health care for as long as I can remember. He should be thrilled, and instead he seemed like he had come to break the news to me that he was going off to war or something.

"We'd be living at the Shahalba Center," Mom continued. "It's a chance to learn meditation techniques from the very best in the world."

I had sudden insight into what was up. My parents wanted us to pick up and move to some granola hippie camp where everyone would be praying to their muse, chanting, and eating a strict vegan diet. Great. Why couldn't my parents be happy in the suburbs like everyone else?

"What's the school like?"

My dad looked confused. "There isn't a school."

"How am I supposed to finish high school?" My parents are really smart, but not great at the common sense stuff. Maybe they thought colleges would accept me based strictly on how Zen I was, no high school diploma needed.

My mom sat down next to me on the bed and petted my knee. "The Shahalba Center is in the woods of Maine. It's completely off the electrical grid." My mom seemed thrilled by the self-sufficiency of the place, but I could already picture it was going to be a problem if I wanted to bring a hair dryer. My mom was a big fan of the all-natural look, but I didn't go anywhere without my flat iron. "The center has a small farm and grows most of its own food. The closest school is almost fifty miles away."

"So are we going to get an apartment or something halfway?"

My mom and dad exchanged another look, and my stomach went into a sudden free fall. I knew what they had in mind.

"No way."

"We've talked to your grandmother and she would love to have you stay with her for the year," my mom said, as if it were completely reasonable for me to consider moving back there.

"Do you remember what happened, what they did to me?

Do you honestly expect me to go to school there? Why don't you ask me to move in with Lauren?"

"All this negative energy isn't good for you."

"It's not random negative energy, Mom. I hate her. I hate Terrace. I don't want to live there."

"And that may be exactly why the universe is bringing you this opportunity. It's a chance to heal, to come full circle." My mom made a large circular motion with her hands, her silver rings flashing in the light.

"This isn't the universe. This is you and dad deciding you want to chant for a year."

"It's more than chanting," my dad said, as if that was the point. Both my mom and I gave him a look, and he stopped talking and went back to scratching his hives.

"Your grandmother is really excited," my mom said.

"What about what *I* want?" I gave a noisy sniff. I wouldn't let them treat me like a five-year-old—easily distracted. *Sure we're ruining your life—but look over here, a shiny grandma!* Hell no. I wasn't falling for it.

"This is a huge opportunity for your dad and me. Living at a center like this is something that we've always wanted to do, and now the school is offering the funding to make this possible. You don't need to be afraid of Lauren."

"I'm not *afraid* of Lauren," I said. I loathed her, but I wasn't afraid. What else could she possibly do to me?

"You should walk back there with your head high. Heck, I

doubt any of those kids would even recognize you now," my dad said.

"Nice way of saying I used to be fat." I turned and faced the wall resting my head against the cool plaster. Trapped.

"I didn't mean you were fat. It was more your old nose I was thinking about," my dad said.

"Great, so I was fat with a big nose. This conversation is doing wonders for my ego."

"What your dad is saying is that you've grown into a lovely young woman. The only power Lauren has over you is what you give her. Hating her just feeds the negative energy. I'm asking you to think the situation over. Grandma is going to give you a call tomorrow morning to talk about it, but if you want my advice, you go back there and you show them that they may have knocked you down, but you didn't stay down."

"What if I think about it and decide I still don't want to do it? What if I want to skip the whole holding my head high thing and instead stay right here and feed my negative energy?"

My mom gave a tired sigh, no doubt thinking I had been switched at birth and somewhere out there was her real child who loved natural fibers, didn't shave her legs, and wasn't difficult about keeping her energy positive.

"We love you. You're the most important thing in our lives. If this is something that you absolutely can't do, then we'll turn down the grant. But before we do that, I want you to think about it, okay?" My dad patted my back a few times before slipping out of the room. My mom took a deep cleansing breath and walked out after my dad.

I could hear my bedroom door shut quietly behind them. Great, a one-way ticket to Guilt Trip. I could either ruin my parents' dream or move to hell's backyard.

I glanced at the full-length mirror on the back of my bedroom door. All around the edges I had taped different pictures—fashion ads from *Vogue*, copies of old vintage movie posters, and some of my pencil drawings. In the upper-right corner, half buried under other photos, was taped a picture of Lauren I'd printed off her Facebook page. I stood up and looked closer at her photo. Lauren hadn't changed much, aside from the black mustache I had drawn on with a Sharpie. She had the same wide smile and strong nose. If you asked me, she was bordering on a horse face. Her hair was longer than in eighth grade, but otherwise I would know her if I saw her.

I looked at myself in the mirror. It had been only three years, but I'd changed a lot. I'd lost thirty pounds the summer I moved. The silver lining of having my life ruined was the stress just melted those pounds off. In New York I walked everywhere and took up yoga. Although I hadn't lost any more weight, what remained, shifted. My braces were gone and I had stopped chewing my fingernails a year or two back. My old nose, as my dad called it, had been a bit beaklike. A year after we moved to New York, I fell down a flight of stairs and landed on my face. I was pretty out of it when they took me to the hospital, but I still had the wherewithal to beg the doctor for a better nose before he put me under for surgery. I may have been raised in an all-natural household, but on my own I had discovered the idea of better living through chemistry—or at least better hair. My former white-girl 'fro of frizzy short hair was now shoulder length, straightened, and highlighted. I had bought a bunch of vintage clothing over the past few years and had my own style. My boobs had also finally showed up. I wouldn't go so far as to say I was hot, but I looked pretty darn good.

I stood straighter and pulled my shoulders back. It was quite possible that my old classmates wouldn't even recognize me, especially since they weren't expecting to ever see me again. Out of sight, out of mind.

Chapter Six

There is nothing normal about my family. You would never see a picture of us in the encyclopedia under "typical family." My parents don't worry about normal parent stuff, like what time I come home at night or my grades. They worry I might buy clothing made in sweatshops and that my love for meat is some kind of character flaw. When I first got my period my mom threw me a "welcome to womanhood party," where she and her hippie, non-armpit-shaving girlfriends got a little drunk on homemade red wine and sang songs about the cycles of the moon. I was the kid in third grade who, instead of bringing cookies to school on my birthday, brought all-natural organic zucchini cupcakes made with applesauce instead of refined sugar. Even the teacher couldn't choke one down.

My grandma doesn't fit the typical grandmother mold either. She doesn't knit or wear sensible shoes. She paints her toenails bright red and wears high heels. She drinks scotch neat and cuts her hair supershort and styles it so it's spiked up in different directions. She looks less like she should be at a bingo parlor and more like she just stepped off a set for MTV. She couldn't be more different from my mom if she tried. You would never know they were related except for the fact that we have the family pictures to prove it. My grandma was the one who got my ears pierced and convinced my parents that a hot dog or two wouldn't kill me.

I sat on the kitchen counter the next afternoon, talking to her on the phone. My parents were in their room so I could have privacy, but I could hear them practically pressed up against the wall trying to hear what I was saying.

"So your folks are going to go off and stare at their navels, huh? I never did get that 'learning how to breathe' thing. Comes natural to me, in and out, regular as clockwork. Given how dumb some people are, you would think more people would just keel over dead if breathing had to be learned."

"Yeah."

"Come on now, I know this place isn't as great as New York, but I've got cable and I'll let you order pepperoni pizza. We'll even get real cheese instead of that soy crud your mom buys."

"It's not that. It's school."

"Is this about that snot Lauren?" she asked. One thing I like about my grandma is she doesn't worry about negative energy; she just calls things as she sees them. "I never was crazy about her. She was a pushy kid, even as a toddler. And her parents? They're so busy social climbing it's a wonder they don't have nosebleeds and a fleet of Sherpas trailing them."

"My parents say the universe is giving me a chance to come full circle, that this is an opportunity."

"Might be on to something."

"Huh?" My mouth dropped open. Was my grandma finally going hippie? Had my mom worn her down with all the talk of chi over the years?

"Look, I don't think the girl is worth another thought, but it's clear she's still stuck in your craw. If she's bugging you that much, then you should do something about it instead of stewing. You'll be going away to college soon. You need to lighten your load."

"Get her out of my craw, so to speak."

"Exactly. Maybe the universe wants you to come back here to teach her a lesson. Lord knows the girl could use it. You know I'm crazy about your mom and dad, but I'm thinking karma could use a helping hand. "

I didn't say anything. I just thought about what she'd said. That was the first time it occurred to me that instead of just thinking about revenge, dreaming about it, I could actually make it happen. Lauren would never see it coming. She would never expect it.

I hung up with my grandma and went back to my room. I pulled the picture of Lauren off my mirror and stared into her face. Revenge didn't have to be a daydream. It could be reality. All it would take was a bit of planning. I could screw her just the same way she screwed me. Maybe my parents were right and it was time to move back. I crumpled up Lauren's picture and tossed it into my trash can. Nothing but net. I went back out to tell my parents the news. Well, part of the news. I kept the bit about the revenge plan to myself.

Chapter Seven

I planned my move back to Terrace with the same level of care and detail employed by nations going to war. My parents, who never met a self-help book they didn't like, were huge fans of goal setting and visualizing your perfect future. How would the universe send you your heart's desire if you weren't clear about what you wanted? I forget which book my mom had gotten it from, *The Secret*, or maybe *Energy for Life*, but she was big on writing down what you wanted. Somehow this was supposed to help the universe bring it to you. The universe apparently has short-term memory loss issues. It needs things written down. My mom was always saying, "The difference between wishing and goal setting is that goal setters have a plan." I wasn't sure I bought into the whole theory, but why take the chance? I thought about every facet of my plan very carefully. I made lists and diagrams. I kept a three-ring binder with all of my notes separated by color-coded tabs. On the first page of my binder I wrote my new mission statement in large block letters so that the universe would be sure to see it, even if the universe had bad eyesight:

GET REVENGE ON LAUREN WOOD

Revenge is a tricky thing. I wanted Lauren to pay, but pay in a very particular way. For example, it might be momentarily satisfying to do one of the following:

1. Push Lauren out in front of a speeding dump truck
2. Slather her with BBQ sauce and set a herd of hungry pit bulls on her
3. Pour honey in her hair and then tie her down on an anthill
4. Dress her in a bathing suit made out of herring and then push her into shark-infested water

However, all of these things would be over quickly. I'll admit it doesn't sound nice, but I wanted her to suffer a bit longer. I wanted her to know what it felt like to have everything taken away. Then there was the added factor that it would be difficult to make a bathing suit out of tiny stinky fish, and I was pretty sure you could do some heavy jail time for pushing people into shark-infested water or into the paths of speeding dump trucks. I wanted Lauren to pay, but I wasn't looking to spend the next forty to life wearing an orange jumpsuit. Orange is so not my color. No, my revenge plan was going to have to be more creative. Plus, I wasn't even sure where I could find a pack of hungry pit bulls.

I made a list of the things that were important to Lauren:

1. Being popular
2. Her boyfriend
3. Getting the lead in the school play
4. Her status as a cheerleader

Once I had the list, the basics of the plan were already framed out. I had to become more popular than she was. I had to steal her boyfriend out from under her, ensure someone else took the lead in the play, and get her kicked off the cheerleading squad.

Now I just had to figure out how to make those things happen.

The popularity angle was going to be the easiest to tackle. High schools have a social structure more strict than a Hindu caste system. By the time you get to your senior year everyone knows exactly where he or she belongs compared to everyone else. You could try to change your status—you could get a new wardrobe or take up a new sport, for example—but it would only take a few days before everyone would shove you back into the place where they felt you belonged. There might be a few people who shifted ranks, but it was highly unusual. I would have the advantage of being a new kid. No one would know exactly where to put me, but they would be trying to sort it out from the first moment they met me. I had to stack the deck. I couldn't *become* popular at Lincoln High. I had to *be* popular from the moment I walked through the front door. I spent hours thinking about what made one person more popular than another. When I was done I taped a list to the mirror in my bedroom so I could study it. It was a thing of beauty.

The Popularity Scale

Attractive: Assign yourself up to 10 points, depending on your level of hotness, zero points being seriously ugly and 10 points being supermodel hot. Bonus 2 points for being fit and in shape versus merely thin. An additional 2 points for hair that looks like a shampoo ad. Minus 1 point if you flip it around way too much. Bonus 3 points for big boobs. Minus 5 points for being attractive but too slutty. Plus 1 point for good use of makeup. Minus 2 points for mild disfigurement such as bad skin, crooked teeth, or bad breath.

Sporty: Assign yourself 5 points for general athletic ability as defined by ability to run without falling over and catching a ball without getting smacked in the face. 5 bonus points for being on key school teams such as football, cheerleading, basketball, or soccer. Minus 2 points for being on dorky teams such as archery or fencing. Bonus 2 points if you have a leadership position on a team. Minus 2 points if you never play and instead always sit on the sidelines.

Rich: Assign yourself 10 points for being filthy rich, 5 points for possessing mere wealth, zero points for being middle class, and minus 5 points for being poor. Bonus point for each item of designer clothing that you own or for accessories such as handbags that cost more than a small used car. Minus 5 points for purchasing your wardrobe at Wal-Mart. Give yourself 2 points if you shop at a funky vintage shop, minus 2 points if you buy your underwear at a thrift store. Some things should never be secondhand.

Cool: Award yourself up to 10 points for exotic factors such as being from a cool place (large city, anywhere in Europe or Hollywood), knowing famous people, having a good car, being in a band (but not *the* band—wearing a uniform that makes you look like a hotel bellman is never cool), or demonstrating artistic ability.

I was going back to Lincoln High, but not as Helen Worthington. I was going to be remade into the destined-to-be-popular Claire Dantes.

I was named Helen after my mom's great aunt. Ever notice you don't meet a lot of Helens these days? That's because it's an old lady name. Thankfully, my middle name is Claire. My mom's maiden name was Dantes, and since I would be living with my grandma it made some sense to borrow it. My mom was ticked that I wanted to register for school under a different name. She said she didn't feel it was necessary for me to hide myself like I was spending my senior year in the witness protection program, but I could tell she was just hurt that I didn't want to use the name she had given me.

In the end my mom backed down. Either my grandma talked her into it or, more likely, the guilt of abandoning me kicked in. No matter the reason—I didn't care—Helen Worthington ceased to exist. Claire Dantes officially registered at Lincoln High. Step one of the plan was in place.

Chapter Eight

It was my grandmother's idea for me to skip the very first day of school. She pointed out the importance of making an entrance. On the first day everyone is hyperexcited, wearing their best new school clothes, squealing when they see people, like they had been separated by the war instead of the summer. She said if I started on the second day, more people would be likely to notice me.

It took everything I had not to skip into the building. My outfit was killer. My hair looked perfect. My plan—foolproof. I could tell just from people's appraising glances as I walked down the hall that I could count on being recognized as destined for popularity before the day was over. I was so excited to finally be doing something versus just thinking about it. I couldn't believe that I had ever hesitated to move back to Terrace. Thank you, universe. I sat in the office waiting for the secretary to give me my locker combination, my foot tapping on the floor.

"Okay, here we go," the secretary said, with that fake cheery voice people use for small kids and the demented elderly. I took the locker combination out of her hand and started to turn. "Wait a minute. Your buddy isn't here."

"Buddy?"

"We provide a buddy to all new students here at Lincoln. She'll make sure you find your classrooms, introduce you to people, and help you feel at home," the secretary said in the same singsong voice.

"You know, I think I'm fine, so I don't need a buddy, but thanks anyway."

"Oh, here she is now. Brenda, this is Claire. You've lucked out, Claire. Brenda is one of our star students here at Lincoln."

Brenda may have been a star student, but I was willing to bet she wasn't popular. Her hair had no layers and came down at an angle, making her head look like a fuzzy, brown Christmas tree. She didn't wear any makeup, and her glasses made her eyes look buggy. She dressed like she borrowed her clothes from a frumpy elderly librarian who had a fetish for the color beige. I had a sneaking suspicion her favorite show was something like *NOVA* or another PBS series. I'm sure Brenda was a lovely person, but she was going to be a big barrier to my popularity project. I needed to ditch her ASAP.

"Here you go!" The secretary stuck a name badge with bright red letters on my shirt: HI! MY NAME IS CLAIRE AND TODAY'S MY FIRST DAY! Brenda was wearing a badge that proudly declared: LINCOLN

HIGH BUDDY! SAY HI TO MY NEW FRIEND, CLAIRE! I stared down at the label on my boob as if some type of disgusting insect had landed there. "You have a great day now," the secretary chirped.

I followed Brenda out of the office. She didn't seem to mind the giant name tag at all. Maybe she thought it was an accessory— fashion didn't appear to be her thing.

"Your locker is down this way," Brenda said as she took off down the hallway. She walked as if she were heading into a windstorm, head down, shoulders squared, her torso thrust slightly forward. She plowed through the crowds of students, a woman on a mission. While she walked, her hands made spastic gestures as she pointed out different things and offered advice: "The gym is down that way. There are water fountains in every wing and also bathrooms. Cell phones aren't allowed in class, so if you have one, you should leave it in your locker. The only class we have together is biology. Do you like science?"

"I guess," I mumbled, trying to look like I wasn't actually with her.

Brenda stopped suddenly and I nearly slammed into her back.

"It's my absolute favorite subject," she stated as if she thought I was going to argue with her, maybe debate the merits of science versus English lit. "What's yours?"

"I don't know. Art, I guess."

Brenda's eyebrows scrunched together. I should point out that her eyebrows didn't have far to go to meet in the middle.

I suspected she didn't consider art to be a real subject. When I didn't say anything else, she headed back down the hall.

Brenda stopped in front of my locker and then stood to the side as if she were my Secret Service agent, prepared to take a bullet for me. Nice girl, but Brenda had to go.

"You know, I appreciate your helping me find my locker and all, but I don't need a buddy."

"The buddy code says that we stick with you for your first week. We give you a tour, make sure you find your classes, help you meet all your teachers, introduce you to our friends, and eat with you at lunch." She ticked each item off on her fingers.

"There's a code?"

"I don't want to get into trouble or anything."

"You're not a big rule breaker, are you, Brenda?"

"No, not really."

"Here's the thing—I think I'll do better on my own." Brenda's eyes widened. I suddenly had the feeling that when she got the call about me coming to town and her chance to be a buddy, it had been the most exciting thing to happen to her in months. "I mean it's not you; it's totally me. I'm the independent type. I'm not really a buddy kind of person." She had no idea how true it was that being buddies didn't come easy to me.

"It's not just the buddy code. I'm also hoping to put this on my transcript so I can show some community service activities. The problem is, we don't get a lot of new students, so if I don't get to help you, then I can't really put it on my applications."

Great, now I was standing between Brenda and her college dreams. Why couldn't she feed the homeless or something? There must be a diseased kitten farm or something where she could volunteer.

"Okay, look, you can show me around and stuff, but we don't need to do the full buddy program thing. Like the name tags, for example."

"You don't like the name tags?" Brenda fingered the edge of her tag.

"No. I hate name tags. It feels like a label. I hate to label people. Isn't part of the buddy code making sure I feel at home?" Brenda nodded. "I don't feel at home in a name tag."

"I guess we could get rid of them."

I ripped the tag off my shirt, crumpled it, and tossed it into my locker. Brenda looked around as if she expected a SWAT team to come and take me down for name tag violations. I pointed at her chest and the offending tag. She sighed and pulled it off. The morning bell gave its first warning.

"Okay, I should get going. I've got French." I dumped a few things in my locker, slammed it shut, and started to head off. "I'll catch you later."

"Wait a minute. How do you know where to go?"

I stopped short. Shit. This was supposed to be my first time in the building. The revenge plan wasn't going to go very well if I couldn't even fool buddy Brenda.

"Just a guess. It felt like French would be that way." I motioned vaguely down the hall.

"Well, you guessed right." Brenda looked like she wasn't sure if she should believe me or not. "Do you want me to walk you down there?"

"No, I'll be fine."

"So, I'll see you later?"

"You bet, buddy!" I gave her what I hoped was a friendly smile and started down the hall. I shot a look behind me and noticed that she was still watching me. What kind of person volunteers to show new people around? With any luck she would settle for giving me a quick tour and then go back to hanging out with her own friends, who no doubt included the president of the chess club.

I slipped into the classroom and gave a quick look around. At the back of the room sat Bailey and Kyla. I recognized them from Lauren's Facebook page as two of her best friends. Of course their matching blue and white cheerleader skirts were also a giveaway. Cheerleader outfits are like gang colors, a sure way to identify who belongs and who doesn't. I didn't talk to anyone, just sat down in an empty desk and stared straight ahead. I had practiced this cool and aloof expression in the mirror until it was perfect. I was wearing a vintage lace shirt under a short black jacket with slim black pants. I'd used a skinny plaid men's tie as a belt. I'd done my best to modify my wardrobe to ride the line between edgy and popular. I peeked down to make sure there wasn't any sticky glue from the name tag still on my shirt.

"*Bonjour*, everyone," Mrs. Charles said tapping on her desk for attention. She looked over at me with a smile. "We have a new student joining our Lincoln High family. I'm sure everyone will welcome"—she paused to look down at her class register—"Claire Dantes. It says you're from New York City. This must be quite the change for you."

I heard people in the room perk up, just as I knew they would. Someone from New York was infinitely cooler than someone who moved from Wisconsin or North Dakota. Granted, we hadn't lived right in the city, but it was close enough. Plus, I didn't plan to mention that we lived in the 'burbs. I gave Mrs. Charles a smile.

"This is senior French. We can test you later to see how what you learned in your old school compares to here, but I'm sure the students here can help you if you need anything."

"*Merci, Madame Charles. J'attends avec impatience vraiment cette classe.*" I looked out over the room. "*J'ai hâte aussi de rencontrer tout le monde.*"

Mrs. Charles's mouth dropped open in surprise.

"You speak lovely," she sputtered, looking down at her class notes as if there would be some additional information there, like that I was secretly a French exchange student or former Bond girl.

"My family spends our summers in France," I said with a

shrug. This was not technically true, but we did spend two weeks there one summer. My dad was fluent, and he and I used to practice by speaking French at dinner. I was willing to bet my French was better than Mrs. Charles's. Besides, summering in France was worth several bonus points on my Popularity Scale with a triple bonus score for being fluent in a cool language.

"You spend your summers in Paris?" Bailey asked, leaning forward on her seat.

"Usually just a few days at the beginning and the end of the trip. You know how it is; Paris is so hot and gross in the summer," I said. Bailey nodded. "We spend most of our time on the Riviera." I gave Bailey and Kyla a smile and turned around so they couldn't see me rubbing my hands together in evil glee.

When class was over I took my time getting my stuff together. As expected, Bailey and Kyla were waiting for me by the door. I tossed my purse over my shoulder, making sure they got a good look.

"Is that a Fendi bag?" Kyla said, eyeing it as if it were sirloin and she was starving.

I spun the bag around and looked at it as if I was noticing it for the first time.

"This? Oh yeah. I got it in New York." I left off the part where I bought it as a knockoff from a street vendor. Let her think I had a few spare thousands to spend on handbags, and that it was the real thing.

"It's gorgeous!" Bailey cooed, running her finger down the side of the bag like it were a baby's cheek.

"Thanks."

"I like your whole outfit," Kyla said.

"London flea market," I tossed off casually.

"You're going to hate shopping here. There's, like, nothing but a total fashion wasteland out here," Bailey offered sadly.

"It's just a year. I'm moving right after graduation."

"Back to New York?"

"Probably, or I'll take a year and backpack through Europe."

Bailey and Kyla looked at each other. I had the feeling they were planning on being roomies at Michigan State, then being the maid of honor in each other's wedding, and most likely would buy houses on the same block. Even though this is what they wanted, they *wanted* to want something else.

"Do you have first or second lunch?" Bailey asked.

"First."

"Awesome. We usually sit over by the windows. Come find us and we'll introduce you to everyone."

I felt a smile slide across my face. It was even easier than I'd hoped.

"Why, that would be just great."

Chapter Nine

I felt nauseated as soon as I walked into the cafeteria, and not just because of the way it smelled. This would be the first time I saw Lauren. Although I was pretty sure my former BFF wouldn't recognize me, I still wondered. We certainly had enough past history. We spent thousands of nights at each other's houses as kids. Her family took me with them on summer vacations. We knew all of each other's secrets. I felt like she should know me even if I looked completely different, and yet at the same time I was counting on her not recognizing me.

The cafeteria at Lincoln High was a mini–solar system of popularity. The most popular kids sat by the windows near the fresh air and light. Even the tables and chairs were nicer in that section. Circling out from there were the hangers-on, the second tier, those who didn't set the trends, but who were the first to carry them out. Then the third tier, those who weren't popular, but weren't unpopular either. And in the final ring, the untouchables, the geeks, the dorks, the stoners, and the losers. Everyone knew their places as well as if there were assigned seats or name cards.

At the very center of the universe, where no doubt she felt she should be, was Lauren. She was the sun; everyone basked in her light. They would be nothing without her. People circled around her like satellites.

I grabbed a salad (popular girl food) from the café lineup and tried to work up the guts to go over to Lauren's table. Kyla saw me and gestured that I should join them. I noticed Lauren still talked with her hands. They waved around as if she were directing an orchestra or guiding in low-flying aircraft. I could see that her nails were painted neon pink. I walked over and stood at the end of their table.

"Hey, there you are! Good thinking not getting the hot option. It's disgusting," Kyla said, making room for my tray.

Lauren was looking at me. I felt my throat tighten. Her head tilted slightly to the side as she inspected me.

"Lauren, this is Claire. She's from New York!" Bailey seemed to be the social secretary in charge of introductions.

"Hey," I said.

Lauren gave a hair flip. I flipped mine. Lauren's nose was scrunched up slightly as if she was considering something very profound, or maybe she was trying to figure out why I seemed familiar to her. I reminded myself to breathe.

"Sit down," Kyla said. "I was just talking about how I have

Mr. Weltch, who everyone calls Mr. Wretch, for anatomy and phys ed. I swear he gets off on cutting stuff up for class. I bet if the police raided his place, they would find a basement filled with the corpses of tortured frogs. He even breathes heavy when he talks about dissection."

"Anatomy is gross," Bailey added to the discussion.

"Yeah, but Tony Mathis is in my class, so things aren't all bad." Kyla turned to me. "Total eye candy. I'll point him out later."

"Do you have a boyfriend?" Lauren asked, finally speaking to me.

"Today's my first day, give me a week or two." For a beat no one said anything, and then Lauren laughed.

"I meant back in New York," she clarified.

I shrugged. "I dated a few guys who went to Columbia, but nothing long-term. I hate to be tied down."

"Well, then don't go out with Mike Weaver, I hear he likes the tie-down thing," Kyla offered, and we all laughed. "If you have any questions on the guys here, just ask us."

"There was this one guy hitting on me, but I don't know. He seems sort of white bread," I said.

"White bread?"

"Looks good, but no substance," I said.

"Who was he?" Lauren asked.

I looked around the cafeteria and spotted my victim.

"There he is, over by the soda machine." I pointed out Justin. An awkward silence fell over the lunch table. I widened my eyes and tried to look innocent. "What? Does he have a reputation, or a disease or something?"

"Uh, no. I mean, he's, uh . . ." Bailey's voice trailed off.

"That's Justin. He's my boyfriend," Lauren said, her lips set in a firm line.

"Oh, sorry." I picked at my salad for a beat. "I'm probably blowing the whole thing out of proportion. Most likely he was just being nice."

"Justin is totally nice," Bailey stressed. Kyla nodded her head in tandem.

I popped a cherry tomato in my mouth and chewed. Poor Justin. Nothing erodes a relationship like some distrust. I mentally placed a check next to the boyfriend-stealing column.

"There you are," a voice said behind me. Kyla's nose wrinkled up like she smelled something bad. I turned around and Brenda was standing there holding her lunch tray, which looked like it had an extra heaping portion of the beef stew. "We're supposed to eat lunch together. I waited for you by your locker."

"Oh, sorry," I said.

"We can still eat together if you want." Brenda looked at the other girls. "I'm her assigned buddy."

"Wow. Assigned friends. Neat," Lauren said.

"It's one of our service programs," Brenda explained. She looked like she couldn't tell if Lauren was making fun of her or not.

"Lincoln High should be proud," Lauren said. "It's students like you who make us such a happy family."

"Thanks," Brenda said. I wanted to crawl under the table on her behalf. Why in the world did she come over here? Kyla gave a quiet snicker.

"I guess you don't want to eat lunch together then, huh?" Brenda asked.

"You know, I'm almost done so it doesn't make much sense." We both glanced down at my tray still piled high with salad, a full drink cup, and an apple.

"Yeah," Brenda murmured, shuffling off, her head down again. She walked as if the lunch tray weighed at least a thousand pounds.

"Catch you later," I said softly, but she didn't turn around.

"God, there's a buddy program? How could I guess that Brenda Bauer would sign up for it? It's like her best chance to make friends." Lauren broke off a piece of her rice cake to eat it.

"She doesn't have any friends?" I asked. I had assumed she had her own crowd.

"She used to hang with some other nerdy girl, I can't remember her name, who moved away at the end of last year."

"So she just hangs out on her own?"

"Her and the voices she hears in her head. She's seriously weird if you ask me," Lauren said.

"What is with her hair anyway? How is it possible to have hair that bad?" Kyla added. "It's like she must deep-fry it to get it that dried out."

"She's been really nice to me," I said. I mentally kicked myself under the table. Sticking up for Brenda was not part of the plan.

"Oh, I'm sure she's really nice," Lauren said, before dismissing Brenda's existence altogether. "So, Claire, are you going out for any school activities?"

"I'm not really sure. At my old school my friends and I didn't do a lot of organized activity stuff." I gave a hair flip, trying to look like I was above school activities. Let them think I hung out at nightclubs or other big-city diversions that weren't even possible here.

"Well, if you're interested, you should check out the drama club. The school musical is huge. We go all out with professional sets and costumes. We're doing *My Fair Lady* this year. It's going to be great."

"You are going to make the best Eliza," Bailey told her, and then looked over at me. "Lauren has had a major part every year, even freshman year when no other freshman was even in the play."

"There's no guarantee on anything," Lauren said. "I don't know who else might try out." She looked over at me with a raised eyebrow.

"Well, you don't have to worry about me. I can't sing. I sound like a reject audition for *American Idol*. You know, the ones they air just for laughs?"

"I can't sing either," Bailey said softly, as if to assure me that my lack of ability was okay, in fact preferred, so that there would be no chance of getting in the way of Lauren.

"Do you want to be a professional actress?" I asked, facing Lauren.

"Oh, I don't know. I mean, it's fun, but the business is so difficult if you want to pursue it as a career." Lauren waved her hand dismissively.

"But you're so good! I mean you are way better than most of the people on TV. I can totally see you walking the Oscar red carpet," Bailey gushed. I wondered if her lips chapped from the amount of ass kissing she did.

"Duh, Bailey, theater stars don't go to the Oscars, they go to the Tony Awards," Lauren said, and I saw Bailey's face flush red hot in embarrassment. "Anyway, I'm not sure about making acting my career. I've thought about majoring in theater in college and giving myself more time to think about it. It's important to keep my options open, but I would never skip college and go straight to Broadway. I wouldn't want anyone to think I went into acting because I couldn't get through college."

Right. God forbid you follow your dreams—what if people think that's the best you could do? I only half listened to Lauren talking about the pros and cons of different theater programs and instead looked around the cafeteria to see if I could spot Brenda. There was no way she could have eaten all that stew so quickly.

I pushed back from the table. Lauren stopped talking,

looking surprised. I had the sense she was used to people hanging on her every word. Well, it was time for her to get used to a new reality.

"Sorry, I've got to go." The three of them looked up at me. My brain scrambled around for a good excuse. "I told my friends in New York that I'd give them a call. We used to have lunch every day at this sushi joint near Times Square, and this is the first time I won't be there." I give a halfhearted shrug. "I told them I would let them know how things are going here."

"God, it must suck having to start over senior year," Bailey sympathized.

"I was really hating it, but I have to say I feel so much better after meeting you guys today. I was afraid I wouldn't meet anyone cool."

Lauren's smile spread slowly across her face and both Bailey and Kyla sat up straighter. Flattery will get you everywhere. Add this to the secrets of popularity: Popular girls are insecure. They act like they aren't, but they are, and a bit of kissing up never hurts.

"Give me your number. We go out all the time. We'll text you and let you know where to meet up with us next time if you want," Kyla said.

"That would be great." I scribbled my number down and passed it over to them. I could tell the people at the tables around us were paying attention to the exchange. Lincoln High's caste system was looking to slot me where I belonged. The way I was dressed helped, and being from New York was a bonus for sure, but what was slotting me into place more than anything else was the fact that the three most popular senior girls wanted to hang out with me. It wasn't even the end of lunch and the popularity project was already a success.

Chapter Ten

I pushed open the bathroom door and heard a juicy sniffle and then silence. I peeked under each of the stall doors. Only the last one had anyone in it—brown, lace-up shoes that looked like they belonged on an orphan in a Third World country. I knew it.

I heard the smothered sound of a choked-back sob. There is no dignity in having a good cry in a public bathroom. My stomach sank as I remembered what the last two weeks of my eighth grade year had been like. I tapped on the stall door with a fingernail.

"Brenda?" I asked softly. She didn't say anything, but I heard another sniffle from behind the stall door. "Brenda, I know it's you. I recognize your shoes. Are you okay?"

"Uh-huh."

My eyebrows went up in disbelief. Brenda was a lousy liar.

"You're not okay. You're crying."

"Just leave me alone."

"Look, I'm sorry about the lunch thing. I should have waited for you at my locker."

Brenda didn't say anything.

"I met those girls in one of my classes and they invited me to eat with them."

"And you would rather eat with them than me. It's fine. I understand. I totally understand."

"You don't understand. There is way more going on than you're imagining. It has nothing to do with you."

"It never does," she said, and then gave a loud blow on her nose.

"Look, come out of there so we can talk."

"No."

I tapped on the door a bit more firmly this time. "You have to come out, classes are going to start."

"I don't have to do anything," she said.

"You're supposed to be my buddy, Brenda. Locking yourself in the bathroom and refusing to talk to me is almost certainly against the buddy code."

"Stop making fun of me."

"I'm not making fun of you. I'm trying to apologize, but it's sort of hard to do talking to a bathroom door."

"Fine, you've apologized. You can go now."

I backed up and leaned against the sink, thinking over my options:

1. **Leave Brenda**. I just met the girl. It wasn't my responsibility to make sure she was okay. I was here for revenge, not to be the Mother Teresa for unpopular girls.
2. **Do something nice**. It wouldn't kill me to be nice to her. It wasn't that long ago that I was the one crying in the bathroom. Besides, no one could see us in here. It wasn't like she was going to derail my popularity plan.

I sighed and got down on my knees, then lay down on the cool tiles and slid my head under her stall door. Brenda looked down at me. Her eyes were red and swollen.

"What are you doing?" she sputtered. For a second I thought she might step on my face as if I were a bug, but instead she scooted over so she was as far away from me as she could get without climbing onto the toilet.

"You don't think I'm serious. I really am sorry. I'm lying on a disgusting bathroom floor so I can show how sorry I am. My hair is touching the floor, Brenda."

"What if someone comes in here?"

"Then no doubt they will call us weirdos for the rest of the year. I'm taking a lot of risks here."

"What do you want?"

"Come out of the stall so we can talk."

Brenda gave me another long look and then unlocked the stall door. Thank God. I stood, brushing off my pants. I went over to the sink and washed my hands. Brenda leaned against the towel dispenser, a long trail of toilet tissue clutched in one hand. She gave a hiccupping sigh, and as she exhaled, a giant snot bubble grew at the end of her nose. It just sat there like a soap bubble perched at the end of her nostril. She didn't seem to notice it was there. It was the saddest thing I could imagine. I took the tissue out of her hand and blotted her nose and then tossed it in the trash.

"It was wrong of me to blow you off today. I never meant to make you feel bad."

"They like you. I could tell. They're the most popular girls in our school."

"I figured. They got the look, you know?"

"Yeah." Brenda went back into the stall and grabbed another wad of tissue, giving her nose a huge blow. She washed her face in the sink and I handed her some paper towels. She tucked her hair behind her ears.

"Wait a minute," I said fishing around in my bag. I pulled out some MAC lip gloss and handed it over. She looked at it as if she had never seen such an item before.

"Put some on."

"My mouth?" She peered at the end of the wand with distrust.

"I don't have rabies or anything. Trust me, it'll look nice."

She put a quick smear on and handed it back. We both looked at her in the mirror. She looked better; the shiny pink lip gloss gave her some color. Of course she was bound to look better without the snot bubble; everything else from there was a bonus.

"Thanks. I guess we're back to being buddies, huh?"

I chewed my lip and tried to figure out how to explain things.

Brenda looked down. "Forget it. This is stupid." She pushed open the bathroom door and left.

I considered going after her, but then I remembered. This was war. There are always risks of civilian casualities.

Chapter Eleven

I'd checked off establish popularity on my to-do list. Now it was time to move to stage two: active destruction.

I had done as much research as possible on Justin, Lauren's boyfriend. I studied his Facebook page as if it held the secret to immortality. I had a piece of paper where I scribbled down every number I thought could be important to him and different combinations of those numbers: Lauren's birthday, their anniversary, his football jersey number, the number of his favorite player on the Detroit Lions, his best track time, and his top score on Grand Theft Auto. I waited until math class was under way with a riveting lecture on the importance of polynomial algebraic functions, and then I raised my hand to request the hall pass.

The halls were empty. I stood outside Justin's locker and wiped my sweaty hands on my jeans. Lincoln High lets you reset your locker combination to anything you like as long as you give the number to the janitor. I was counting on the idea that Justin would pick something he could easily remember. He struck me as the kind of guy who doesn't have a lot of spare storage space in his brain. I tried Lauren's birthday first, nothing. Then their anniversary, nothing. I tapped my foot, thinking what my best chance would be. I'd only known the guy a couple of days. There were zillions of combinations of numbers he could've picked. I worried it would take all year to try them all, and my math teacher would have someone come looking for me long before then. I dialed in his birthday, hoping Justin was a keep-it-simple kind of guy. I spun the lock around, then said a small prayer, and pulled down. Nothing. Shit. In frustration, I yanked harder and then it clicked, popping open. It sounded really loud in the empty hallway and I flinched, waiting for classroom doors on either side to fly open with people pouring out to ask me what the hell I was doing, but nothing happened.

I pulled open the door and took a step back. Ick. At the bottom of Justin's locker was a pile of gym clothing and football gear that smelled like he last washed them sometime around sophomore year. The odor waves were nearly visible to the naked eye. It was possible that there were a few lunch leftovers buried in there too. Something had a vague banana-past-its-prime smell to it. I held my breath and started rummaging around in his jacket pockets. Nothing.

Lincoln High forbids students from having cell phones in class. I was certain Justin would keep his in his locker like everyone else. I gave another quick look around. I didn't have time to do an archeological dig in the compost pile at the bottom of the locker. How did he manage to get so much stuff in here already? I reached my hand up and tried to feel around on the shelf, hoping that I wouldn't grab a hold of anything too nasty since I couldn't see what he had up there. I felt his keys, a tennis ball, and what I desperately hoped was not a jockstrap even though that's what it felt like, and then—BINGO—his phone. I snatched it off the shelf and fought the urge to do a celebration dance. I snapped it open and dialed my own cell number, waited for the call to connect, and then hung up. I slid it back onto the shelf and shut the door.

I made it one step before I snapped back, nearly falling to the floor. It felt like someone had grabbed me around the neck. Shit. My scarf was shut in the locker.

I gave my scarf a tug, but it was caught. I could hear someone walking down the other hall. They were going to round the corner any second. I turned around the best that I could, given that the locker had me in a choke hold, and gave the scarf a yank. It didn't budge an inch. I tried to figure out if I could lean against the door and look casual. Nope. My fingers flew over the lock, spinning in Justin's birth date. It clicked open and I yanked my scarf out, shutting the door an instant before the janitor came around the corner. He looked at me with my hand on the lock and sweat pouring down my face.

"Wrong locker," I said with a nervous laugh. "They all look alike from the outside. How's a person supposed to tell which one is theirs?"

"They're numbered."

I looked at the lockers like I had never seen them before. "Well, look at that, they *are* numbered. That's handy."

The janitor gave me a look and kept going, pushing the AV trolley. I went back to Justin's locker during biology, English, and study hall, and did the same thing, minus the whole getting-my-scarf-caught part. Karma was clearly on my side, because not once did anyone ever see me in his locker and the timing was perfect. When I went back to my locker at the end of the day there was a text message from Lauren letting me know they were meeting up at Bean There Done That after school. I also had a long list of calls from Justin's phone. Perfect.

Chapter Twelve

ean There was a classic Starbucks knockoff—squishy brown sofas pulled up close to a gas fireplace and clusters of scarred wooden tables with tiny bistro chairs scattered around. There were stacks of papers folded open to the entertainment and sports sections on all the windowsills, and the smell of coffee and high-calorie muffins floated through the air. The barista had his black hair tied back and a row of silver hoops marched in lockstep up the side of his ears. He called out the drinks in a singsong voice.

"One large capp-uchiiiiiiiiiii-no." He slid the cup across the counter, confident that it wouldn't go hurling off the edge, and I saw a harried-looking junior girl lunge to grab it before it could slide too far.

I found Lauren and the others at the back of the café. The tables in the back were up a small riser, just slightly higher than the rest of the café. Leave it to Lauren to find a stage wherever she went. Lauren had her feet up on a chair to hold a space for me. Although other people were standing around waiting for tables, I noticed no one even tried to take the chair away from her. I watched them while I waited for my drink. The student body of Lincoln High wandered in and out of Bean There, acting as if it were a privilege to be able to see the great Lauren Wood sip her coffee. And Lauren knew it too. She laughed just a bit too loud and had all these exaggerated hand gestures so that even the folks at the far side of the café wouldn't miss her performance.

"Medium, no foam, skinny, chai laaaaaaaaaaa-te!" I grabbed my drink and after a quick sip, gave the barista a salute with the cup. Always acknowledge perfection. I wove my way through the tables. When Lauren saw me she paused for a second before taking her feet off my chair, just long enough to emphasize what a favor she was bestowing on me. I flopped down and gave everyone a smile. Lauren looked over at my drink.

"Dairy?"

"Chai tea. Want some?" I pushed the drink in her direction, and she pulled back as if I were offering her a nice steaming cup of hemlock.

"I don't touch dairy. It clogs up my vocal cords." She shrugged as if this were a hardship she was used to enduring. "I've still got voice lessons tonight. I'm practicing my song for tryouts."

"So you stick with plain black coffee then?"

"Hot water with lemon."

I nodded and took a long sip of my throat-coating milky tea, fighting the urge to gargle it in front of her.

"Where did you get those boots?" Kyla asked, nearly falling to her knees when she noticed them.

I turned my foot from side to side so everyone could get a good look.

"I think I got them at one of the Manolo sample sales. All the designers in New York do these trunk sales and you can get amazing deals." I bought them at a thrift store, but whatever. Lauren's eyes looked down at them.

"I never liked Manolos. I think they're a bit flashy," Lauren said.

I shrugged. The only thing she didn't like about Manolo shoes was that she didn't own any.

"You can order some great shoes on Zappos online," Kyla said.

"Yeah, but I hate to buy shoes without trying them on, especially when they're expensive, you know?" I said, and we all nodded, acknowledging how it was less than ideal. I pulled my phone out and placed it on the table.

"Waiting for a call?" Bailey asked.

"Someone has been calling all day and hanging up, or worse, sort of breathing heavy. I swear to God, it's driving me nuts. I want to catch it next time it goes off. It's the same number so I know it's the same guy."

"Someone has a secret admirer," Bailey said, and everyone laughed. "Do you know who it is?"

"No idea. On one message there was this 'um . . . um,' like he was trying to say something, but in the end he still hung up."

"You should call him back and ask him if he's worked up the balls to ask you out yet," Kyla suggested.

"Here, give me your phone and I'll call him," Lauren said, snatching my phone off the table. "He might be cute, you never know. I'll tell him you never talk dirty to someone who doesn't speak up."

"Woo!" cheered one of the sophomore boys sitting near us. "You can talk dirty to me anytime." His friends high-fived him.

"In your dreams, Sutherland—you're just a baby. I don't do kiddie porn," Lauren fired back, making everyone laugh.

Lauren flipped her hair and smiled. She looked down at the phone and I watched the blood drain out of her face when she recognized the number. Bailey and Kyla were still swapping comments with the sophomores and didn't notice. Lauren started jabbing at my phone. Kyla yanked her chair closer to the table as if story hour were about to begin and she wanted to be right in the first row.

"So call him. We're ready."

"Don't be a child, Kyla." Lauren tossed the phone back down on the table. "I wouldn't really call him. I don't play games with people. God. Sometimes you act like you're still in junior high."

Kyla pulled back as if she had been slapped. Bailey looked

back and forth between Kyla and Lauren like a small kid watching her parents fight. I picked up the phone and looked at it.

"You deleted the number," I said.

"What, you were going to call him?" Lauren asked.

I shrugged as if I couldn't care less.

"We were just joking around," Kyla said.

"Whatever. If you want to act like that, maybe you should start trolling the junior high so you can find a guy with your sense of humor." Lauren's chair legs squealed on the floor as she pushed away from the table too fast. "I gotta go. I've got to get to my voice lessons." Lauren tossed her tote bag over her shoulder and left without another word.

"Whoa. Who peed in her cornflakes?" Kyla asked.

"She's probably just getting nerves over the whole play thing," Bailey said, looking out the window to watch Lauren walk away. "Tryouts always freak her out and this is her senior year, so the lead means the world to her."

"It doesn't mean she has to take my head off." Kyla took a deep drink of her coffee and then winced from the heat. Her foot bounced up and down.

"Oh, you know she doesn't mean it. Don't be mad. Look, anyone want to share a muffin? I'm starving." Bailey didn't wait for us to answer and instead popped up and headed to the bakery case.

"For what it's worth, you totally didn't deserve that," I said, once Bailey was out of range. Step two: divide and conquer.

"Oh, Bailey's right. Lauren doesn't mean anything by it. It's just sometimes, she's . . . you know . . ."

"I know. A bunch of my friends in New York acted just like Lauren. I mean, they don't call them drama queens for nothing."

Kyla met my eyes with surprise, and then we both burst out laughing.

"Hey, what size shoe do you wear?" I asked, pointing at her feet.

"They're huge aren't they? They're eight-and-a-halfs."

"I have flipper feet too—curse of being tall. Do you want to borrow these boots? You can have them for the weekend if you want."

"Are you serious? You would lend them to me?"

"Of course. They're just boots. It's not like I'm giving you a kidney or anything."

I bent over to slide one off and passed it over. "Try it on and see if it fits."

Kyla gave a squeal, kicking off her shoe and pulling on the boot. She held her foot out in front of her, turning it this way and that. Bailey came back with a muffin cut in three equal pieces. I had a suspicion Bailey would end up working as a nursery school teacher in the future.

"Check it out—Claire's lending me her boots!"

"Oh my God, that's so nice."

I gave them both a smile. That was me. Nice.

Chapter Thirteen

*B*renda called the next night. She'd used her buddy status to weasel my phone number out of the secretary. So much for privacy. She said she wanted to check in on me and make sure I was settling in okay. I admire tenacity in other people. However, I had my own project that required my focus. On the other hand, being nice to Brenda (at least when no one was watching) would balance out my own karma just in case my parents were right on that angle. I would destroy Lauren, but maybe if I built up Brenda, then in some way the whole thing evened out. I went ahead and accepted her invitation to come over.

Brenda's room was painted an icy blue. Her bed was shoved off in the corner, and the bulk of the room was taken up with a large desk and floor-to-ceiling bookshelves. I stood in front of her closet, sliding the hangers back and forth, hoping for her sake that she was hiding the good stuff in the back.

"I dress more for comfort than style," Brenda said, picking at her cuticle. I took a swipe at her hand.

"You don't say. Did you buy every item of clothing you own from Eddie Bauer?"

"What's wrong with Eddie Bauer?"

"Do you ever look at their catalogs?" I asked, and Brenda nodded. "When you look at the pictures do you notice a lot of hot people our age cavorting about?"

"No." She lifted her hand toward her mouth and saw me staring so she put it back down on the bedspread.

"Correct. You see pretty middle-aged women with good skin. Eddie Bauer's target audience is the suburban mom who wants to look nice, but needs pants that don't have to be ironed and repel stains. Eddie Bauer spends zillions of dollars on advertising. They're telling you in their ads who they are trying to attract. It's not the youth market."

"I'm not the kind of person who wears skintight jeans and crop tops."

I gave a sigh and sat down on the floor in front of her. "You are aware that there are options other than a khaki collection or slut wear?"

"I'll keep it in mind if I ever decide to redo my wardrobe."

"If you're thinking redo, you should tackle your hair first."

Both Brenda and I turned so we could see her reflection in the mirror above her dresser. Her hair seemed to come straight out of her head, giving her the overall appearance of a triangle.

"Where do you get your hair cut?"

"Supercuts at the mall."

"Here's some free advice. You don't have to spend a lot of money to be popular, but you have to spend your money wisely. For example, don't spend wads of cash on underwear. Most people won't see it, and anyone who does will be trying to get you out of it so they won't care. You can buy underwear at Target. However, your hair is a different story."

"What makes you think I need advice on how to be popular?"

I raised an eyebrow. "It's not about being popular, it's about how to play the game."

"I don't care about that stuff."

"Yes you do. Trust me. Everyone cares. Your hair is a giant billboard on your head. Your billboard is saying: 'I've never heard of deep conditioner and I spend seven dollars on haircuts.'"

"They cost fourteen dollars."

"Still not impressed. Toss me the phonebook and I'll make you an appointment."

"I hate fancy salons."

"Tough. With your type of hair, you've got two options: You get a good cut and then use a straightening iron in the mornings and avoid damp weather conditions, or you get your hair cut in layers and let it curl up a little. Trust me, I understand bad hair. You should have seen mine before I did a major intervention on it. How much time do you spend on your hair in the mornings now?"

"I don't know. I take a shower and stuff."

"Basic hygiene doesn't count. I think we should go with curly. It'll be easier for you to keep up. And we need to lose some of the length, something fun and flirty."

I made a call to the salon and asked to talk to the stylist directly. I described exactly the look I had in mind, as I could tell this was not the kind of thing to leave in the cuticle-chewed hands of Brenda.

She was looking into the mirror when I got off the phone, pondering her reflection.

"Look, popularity is a science. It's not as shallow as it looks."

"Really?" Brenda crossed her arms.

"Popularity is a mathematical formula based on desirability criteria. High schools are a classic anthropological case study, and getting people to respond in the way you want is psychology. All science. It's just not the type of science that you're used to."

"I can't figure you out. You don't seem like the other popular girls I know."

"God, I hope not. I'm shooting to have a bit more depth. Lauren is as shallow as a kid's wading pool with a leak."

"I don't get it. If you don't like her, why do you want to be her friend?"

"It's complicated." I looked at my watch. "I gotta go. You'll get your hair done on the weekend and then you'll see: science."

As I bounced out of the house I felt my karma balance out with what I was going to do tomorrow.

Chapter Fourteen

"Your parents sent you something," my grandma said as I walked in the house. She was in the kitchen drinking a glass of wine and flipping through *Bon Appétit*. "Should we make a cake or something? There's a recipe in here for turtle brownies."

"Sure." I sat down at the counter and opened the box from my folks. The box had large grease stains on it. Inside was a square of some type of baked good. It looked like it had twigs baked into it, and it weighed a zillion pounds. I gave it a sniff. It was hard to describe the smell, but the word "good" wasn't even close to making the list.

"What is that?"

I looked at the note my parents included. "It's a sugar-free high-fiber protein bar. It has fish oil in it." We both looked down at the box.

"Who makes brownies out of salmon?"

"You want to make them out of turtles," I countered.

My grandma laughed and then looked at the box again. "You going to eat that?"

"Are you going to make me?"

"I'm pretty sure that would count as child abuse. I'm too old to do prison time. Do me a favor and don't put it in the kitchen garbage; take it directly to the garage. That's the kind of smell that sticks around." She started pulling things down from the kitchen cupboards. "You look mighty happy with yourself. I take it the whole going to school with Lauren thing is working out okay?"

"So far so good. I'm putting stage two of my revenge plan into place."

My grandma looked at me over her shoulder with her eyebrows raised. "Revenge plan?"

"Yeah. Basically I'm going to ruin Lauren's life, like she did mine."

"Honey, she didn't ruin your life."

"She sure tried. High school is supposed to be the best time of my life and look at me. Do I look like I'm having the time of my life?"

"I never trust people who had the best time of their lives in high school. That's not the point. If you haven't done what you wanted with your life then it's up to you to change it."

"I'm working on changing it."

"Sounds like you're working on changing *her* life, not yours."

I stood up, pushing the box from my parents away from me. The day had gone perfectly and now this.

"You were the one who gave me the idea. You said I should seize the opportunity."

"I meant come back here and show them who's boss. Prove to yourself that you're fine. You're pretty, you're smart, and you have more artistic skill in your little finger than most people do in their whole bodies. I didn't mean that you should go around trying to put some kind of half-baked revenge plan into place."

"It's not half-baked!" I yelled, and both my grandma and I took a step back in surprise at my voice.

"Okay." My grandma wiped the already clean counters. "Look, sit down again for a minute."

I sat down with my arms crossed.

"Maybe what I said when we talked about you moving out here got lost in translation. That's the problem with doing all your deep talking on the phone." She ran her hands through her hair. "Lauren is what my generation used to call 'a real piece of work.' She doesn't deserve to polish your shoes, and I never knew what you saw in her. You can do much better in the friend department. I have no problem with you going back to school with a clean slate and a different name. I think it makes more sense than trying to deal with all that baggage, but the point of a clean slate is that it's clean. If I knew you were going to drag all this mess with you, I wouldn't have gone along with the plan of registering you under another name."

I opened my mouth to protest, but she held up a hand and cut me off.

"You don't have to like her. You don't have to have anything to do with her, but trust me when I tell you that trying to hurt her isn't going to do anything but hurt you."

"You don't think she deserves it?"

"I can think of few people who would deserve it more than she does, but that's not the point. The point is whether you should be the avenging angel. People like her usually get what they've got coming."

"What if they don't?"

"There is usually more going on in people's lives than we know. Maybe her life isn't as good as you think."

"She's popular; she has friends and a boyfriend. She's in the drama group and destined to star in the play. She's captain of the cheerleading team. It's not fair after what she did to me to get there."

"You want revenge? Be happy. Live your life. Make some friends, good friends. Push your talents. Make yourself even better."

"Fine." I picked at the tape on the box and didn't meet her eyes.

"One of the benefits of being an old lady is you get some perspective. I'm not trying to rain on your parade. If I thought destroying her would make you happy, then I'd jump right in and help out, but it won't."

"Okay," I said. I didn't say anything else, as I was pretty sure that if I tried, I would start crying. Instead I pulled the long strip of tape off the greasy box and breathed slowly through my mouth.

"All right then. You get rid of that thing, and I'll get the stuff together, and we'll make ourselves some proper fish-free brownies. I think *Casablanca* is on TV tonight. Chocolate and Bogart, it doesn't get better."

I walked out to the garage and dumped the box into the trash. It wasn't that I didn't appreciate what my grandma was saying; it was just that I thought she was wrong. It could be better than chocolate and Bogart. I wasn't giving up on the revenge plan. I was just getting started.

Chapter Fifteen

*B*renda's hand kept wandering up to touch her hair as if she expected to find it gone. The salon had done a great job. They cut her hair about six inches shorter, so it hung just below her ears with layers all over. With the length gone, her hair had bounced right up into great curly waves—it was a pixie cut with moxie. They put in a semipermanent color just a shade or two warmer than her own natural brown along with what must have been industrial conditioner designed to tame hair that had survived a nuclear blast. I'd also convinced her that wearing lip gloss and mascara would not put her at risk for looking like a Cover Girl dumping ground.

"Stop touching your hair," I said as I paused to look at one of the window displays. Bailey hadn't been kidding when she said this place was a fashion wasteland. It was one chain store after another.

"It's pretty short."

I turned to give her a look. "You cannot tell me that you don't like it."

She reached up to touch it again, tucking a small piece behind her ear. The corners of her mouth pulled up slightly. Then I saw it across the hall.

"That's it, over there." I dragged her by the arm behind me.

"This is a guy store."

I pointed at the crisp, white shirt in the window. "One of those."

"What's wrong with the white shirt I already own?"

"Wrong style." I wandered past her and into the store. I held the shirt out in front of her. "We're going for an Audrey Hepburn–inspired look. You already own about six zillion capri pants, so that's a start, and we'll add a nice black skirt. You've got a great figure—why not use it? We'll make some of your Eddie Bauer cardigan collection work until you can afford to replace them. You need a few men's-style button-down shirts and ballet flats. That should give you enough to mix and match so you have stuff to wear. "

"I don't know." Brenda looked at the shirt doubtfully.

"You're supposed to trust me. Plus the shirt is half off," I said, pointing at the hanger tag. "They are practically giving it away. The Hepburn look suits you. You have similar body types."

"I don't look anything like Audrey Hepburn."

"That's because you're always hunched over. You have lousy posture. You never saw Audrey all hunched up. That reminds me of something else. We need to stop at Best Buy."

"I already asked my dad to rent the movies you recommended. I don't need to buy them."

"First of all, watching Hepburn movies is not a chore, so stop making it sound like I'm making you do chemistry problems."

"I like chemistry," Brenda said.

"You'll like Hepburn. She exudes charisma—that's nature's chemistry," I said, extending my arms for drama.

"I know what charisma is."

"Stop sounding so grumpy. What I want is for you to buy a yoga DVD. It will be good for your posture."

"Yoga?" Brenda rolled her eyes.

"Trust me. Yoga leads to great posture. Now get the shirt."

Brenda took the shirt and marched over to the cash register. If she decided against a career in the sciences she could consider the military with that gait. However, the hair alone was starting to make a difference. Her shoulders were back just a bit, and she looked into the clerk's face instead of at the floor. Progress.

Brenda came back swinging her bag slightly, which for her was practically giddy girly behavior.

I linked arms with her and we headed out into the mall as if we were starring in *The Wizard of Oz* and the yellow brick road led to Best Buy. We were laughing when I saw the flying monkeys.

"Shit," I said, stopping short and ducking into Claire's behind an earring rack. Brenda took a few more steps forward before she realized I wasn't next to her. She stood in the middle of the hallway looking around to see where I went. A few steps away at the Baskin Robbins stood Kyla, Bailey, and Lauren.

"What are you looking at?" Kyla asked.

Brenda pointed to her own chest with a finger.

"Yeah, you," Kyla said, pinning her in place with her words.

"Nothing. I was, uh . . ." Brenda looked around again.

"Great. All I need is people staring at me. Call the circus, my life is a freak show," Lauren cried. A few people in the mall turned around to see the drama.

"Here, have a smoothie," Bailey said, passing over a giant pink concoction.

"I might as well. What does it matter if I gain a thousand pounds? Then I can be fat and alone instead of just alone."

"You guys will work it out," Bailey said, stroking Lauren's arm as if she were a prized Siamese kitten.

"He's a dumb fuck if he doesn't realize what an ass he's being," Kyla offered.

"Is everything okay?" Brenda asked.

"Nothing that concerns you," Kyla said with a hand on her hip.

"She might as well know, because it's going to be all over school on Monday. Justin and I broke up. It's over!"

I nearly sucked in a pair of silver hoops. They broke up! Yes! The plan had worked. I would have done a celebration dance except for the fact I was hiding.

"Justin Ryan the football player?" Brenda asked.

"Duh," Kyla said.

"Three years. You know there are Hollywood marriages that haven't lasted as long as our relationship." Lauren gave a giant suck on her straw, making an unpleasant slurping sound. "Do you know how many other people I could have been going out with in that time? Plenty. Guys ask me out all the time and even guys who haven't asked—I can tell they totally would if they thought they stood a chance."

"Totally," Bailey assured her.

"I'm sorry he broke up with you," Brenda offered.

Lauren spun around and Brenda took a step back.

"Let's be really clear about something, Justin did NOT break up with me. I broke up with Justin. I caught him lying to me and the one thing I will not tolerate is lies." Lauren punctuated each word with a point of her finger. I noticed even from across the hall that her manicure was chipped and one nail was broken off completely.

I gave a snort; apparently she was fine with tolerating her own lies. Karma's a bitch, bitch.

"If you can't trust them, dump them," Kyla offered, and then gave her head a shake before grabbing her own smoothie off the counter. "I still can't believe it. He worships you. What the hell is worth so much to him that he would lie about it?"

"It doesn't matter what he lied about. The point is, he lied. The individual lie is unimportant. Would you stop trying to pump me for information? All anyone cares about is the nasty details." Lauren chucked her smoothie at the trash can. The cup hit the side, bounced off, and crashed to the floor. It spread pink smoothie goo across the floor. "My pain is not for everyone's amusement."

I couldn't speak for the others, but I was finding her pain quite amusing. Lauren stomped off without a look back. The three of them watched her go for a beat and then looked down at the oozing pink smoothie. Bailey was the first to act, grabbing a fistful of napkins from the counter and sprinkling them onto the floor, tapping them down with the toe of her shoe. Kyla took a step back as if she didn't want to be connected to the mess. Brenda asked the counter attendant for a roll of paper towels and began helping Bailey.

"We're supposed to be her best friends," Kyla grumbled. "Wanting to know why she broke up with her boyfriend of three years is not exactly pumping her for information. She acts like I was trying to waterboard her."

"She's just upset," Bailey said, tossing a wad of soggy napkins and paper towels in the trash.

"There's being upset and then there's being a bitch."

I nodded behind the earring rack. Kyla was starting to catch on. I could have told her stories that would make her think calling Lauren a bitch was a compliment.

"We should go after her," Bailey said.

Kyla tossed her hair. "No thanks. I can think of better ways to spend a Saturday. I'm going to go look at makeup. Are you coming?"

Bailey chewed on her lower lip, looking down the hall where Lauren had disappeared.

"Forget it," Kyla said, and started to walk in the opposite direction. Bailey looked ready to cry. Brenda finished mopping up the rest of the smoothie, throwing another large handful of paper towels into the trash, and then wiped her hands off.

"Well, I'll see you around," Brenda said.

Bailey looked at her as if she had forgotten Brenda had been there at all.

"Thanks for helping me clean up," Bailey said.

"No problem."

Bailey started to walk after Lauren and then stopped.

"Did you get a haircut or something?" Bailey asked, looking at Brenda as if she had never seen her before. Brenda's hand wandered up to give her new hair another pat and then nodded.

"It looks nice," Bailey said before heading off after Lauren. I waited a few seconds and then came up behind Brenda. She jumped when I touched her arm.

"Where did you go?" she asked, whipping around.

"Sorry. I didn't want to run into them."

"Well, thanks for letting me wander into that little scene by myself."

"She liked your hair. Did you notice that?"

"You're changing the subject."

I stood looking down the hallway for a beat. There was something about the whole scene that felt wrong. I should be thrilled

Lauren and her boyfriend were busted up. She could say she was the official "breaker upper," but the fact was, from her perspective, Justin cheated on her. He picked someone else. She should be unraveling, falling apart.

"Did you notice Lauren wasn't that upset?" I said.

"She threw a smoothie."

I waved my hand, dismissing it. "Drama. Lauren is an actress. She knows the importance of a good use of props."

"That smoothie was no prop. She seemed upset to me, and her best friends think she's upset."

"One of her friends thinks she's upset. The other one thinks she's being a bitch." I chewed on the inside of my cheek. "Did you notice that she wasn't even crying? Her eyes weren't red either. No stuffy nose. And if they thought she was really upset, would they have brought her to the mall? Doesn't that seem weird?"

"What seems weird is how you're acting about the whole thing," Brenda said.

"What? Admit it, Lauren Wood can be a real cow. Isn't there even a teeny-tiny part of you that sort of enjoys that things are falling apart for her?" I held my fingers and thumb close together and squinted through the hole.

"She's not a friend of mine, but I wouldn't want to see something bad happen to anyone."

I rolled my eyes. "She's not your friend because she would never be your friend. She can't get anything from you, which renders you useless in her book. She wouldn't do a thing to help you out if you needed it, and if she had something to gain by hurting you, she'd do it so fast you wouldn't even see her sneaking up with the knife."

"What did she do to you?"

My lower lip started shaking and out of nowhere I felt like I could burst into tears right in the center of the mall food court. "It doesn't matter." I gave my eyes a wipe. "Let's go get the yoga DVD."

"Sort of seems like it does matter."

I took a deep breath and looked up at the ceiling, trying to pull the tears back into my eyes using willpower. "Forget the whole thing," I said. Brenda had crossed her arms and was looking at me. "As a friend, I'm asking you to drop it."

"Lauren isn't my friend, but it doesn't seem like you're much of a friend either. You don't tell me what's going on, you don't tell me what's important to you, and you don't even want to be seen with me. As soon as we run into someone, you run off. In fact, the only thing you tell me is what to do."

"That's not fair. It isn't that I don't want people to see us together, it's just . . ." My voice trailed off. She was right. I couldn't afford to be seen with her. My popularity was still too tenuous.

Brenda looked away from me and then started to gather up her shopping bags. "Thanks for coming with me to get my hair cut and all the shopping advice. I should head home."

"What about getting a yoga thing?"

"I can manage it on my own. You don't have to hold my hand every step of the way."

"Oh. Okay. I guess I'll see you around."

"And if I'm really lucky you'll even be able to acknowledge that you know me."

"It's not like that," I protested.

"Just because you don't want it to be like that, doesn't mean that isn't exactly what it is." Brenda hiked up her bags, then turned away.

Chapter Sixteen

When we were in third grade, Lauren and I had a thing for Nancy Drew books. We would pretend to be Nancy and her best friend Bess, the crime-solving duo. (Care to guess who got to be Nancy and who was stuck being boring Bess?) We decided we didn't have to pretend. We would open our own detective agency, Wood & Worthington Incorporated. Her name had to go first. After all, she pointed out, it was only fair to go in alphabetical order. We made agency letterhead and business cards on Lauren's dad's color printer. We passed out our cards to neighbors and posted a sign at the Meijer's and waited for the cases to pour in. Not too bad for being eight and a half. Our first mystery, the Case of the Missing Library Book, came from my mom.

My mom was missing a copy of *Veggie Fun*, a vegan cookbook. It was a high-stakes case, because every day that it went unfound the library was raking in another day's fine. Lauren leaned back in my desk chair, balancing one of her pink, glitter spiral notebooks on her lap.

"We should make a list of suspects," Lauren said, spinning the pen between her fingers.

"It could be Ms. Tarton's dog, Peanut. He's always burying stuff in the backyard."

"Mmm-hmm." Lauren wrote Peanut down in her notebook with a big number one by his name. "Does Peanut have any history with books? Any witnesses who might have seen him chewing on a book or something?"

"Not sure." We went back to thinking. Crime solving was a lot more work than it looked like in the books.

"Has he bitten anyone?"

"Peanut? No. He's a really nice dog. Plus he's a wiener dog so he's only like six inches tall. I'm not sure he could bite anything important. He goes to the hair salon most days with Ms. Tarton, so he's not even around most of the time."

"Remember what Nancy says—just because someone looks like they're innocent doesn't mean they are." Lauren waved her finger in my direction. I tried to picture Peanut as a hardened criminal. We each went back to trying to think of another suspect. One thing our neighborhood was missing was nefarious characters. "Maybe we should do a stakeout and try and see if there are any clues."

A stakeout seemed way more fun than hanging out in my room, so we went prowling around the neighborhood. We ended up in the park that backed up to the Tartons' backyard. Peanut was wandering around the yard, barking at birds as they flew through the sky. Peanut was nothing if not an optimist. We got down on our hands and knees so we could sneak up closer to the fence and observe him at close range. It was possible that if he didn't know anyone was watching, he would disclose the secret lair (or hole) where he had hidden the library book.

The leaves rustled as we crawled forward. Lauren looked over her shoulder and gave me a face to be quiet. I almost started giggling because she looked just like her mom did when she would stomp down the hall to Lauren's room and beg us to "Please keep down the volume. This is a home, not a trailer." We weren't really sure what being in a home versus a trailer had to do with anything, but we would always shush up. Lauren's mom wasn't the kind of parent who liked to tell you something twice. That was when it happened. I took another crawl forward putting my hand down in a pile of mud brown leaves. I felt a sudden hot pain in the palm of my hand.

I yelled out and yanked my hand back. Peanut let out a howl and ran over to the fence near us, barking his alert. Sticking out of the palm of my hand was a large carpenter nail buried into the flesh. I knew it was bad, but I knew it was really bad when I saw Lauren's face. Her eyes were wide and she looked a bit nauseated. I pulled the nail out with my other hand and blood welled up and poured down my wrist.

"Oh my gosh," I cried, looking at all that blood, my blood.

Lauren whipped off one of her shoes and scrambled to get her sock. She wound it around my hand, squeezing slightly. I'm not sure they covered sock triage in Girl Scouts, but it worked.

"It's going to be okay. We'll go get your mom."

"She's going to be mad at me."

"No she won't."

"Yes she will," I said, somehow sure this would be the case. I started to cry in tandem with Peanut's howls. I felt a fresh wave of pain with every beat of my heart. Lauren looked around on the ground, kicking at the piles of leaves and then bent down to grab the nail. Without hesitating she stabbed herself in the palm. Her wound wasn't as deep as mine, but it was longer and it started to bleed instantly. I stopped crying and looked at her in shock.

"Now we're in trouble together," Lauren said, grabbing my hand, the bloody sock between our palms giving a squishy noise as we shook. "And we're also blood sisters. That's better than real sisters because we did it by choice instead of just being born that way. So you don't ever need to worry about stuff, because I'll be there. I'll figure out something with your mom. And then some-day you'll do something for me."

I remember thinking at that moment that there was no one cooler than Lauren. I was sure she would be my best friend for-ever. Heck, we were blood sisters. Of course, in fairness, at that age, I thought Pop-Tarts were the height of good cuisine, so it's clear I wasn't a great judge of quality.

My mom drove us both to the emergency room for tetanus

shots. Lauren was in the front seat telling my mom this elaborate story to explain how we both managed to puncture our hands at the same time. My mom didn't seem to be buying it, but she wasn't mad either. She had washed each of our hands out at home and wrapped them in clean dishtowels for the trip to the hospital. I was hoping for stitches because I thought they would make me look cool. I sat in the backseat holding my arm in the air the way my mom had told me too. My mom braked quickly when someone cut in front of her in traffic, and the missing library book slid out from under her car seat.

Case solved. Whatever happened between Lauren and me was still a mystery.

Chapter Seventeen

I lay on my bed, tossing a tennis ball up into the air and catching it. Just another exciting Saturday night. I couldn't tell if the plan was working. Lauren didn't seem to be unraveling as much as I had hoped. I wasn't looking to put her in a bad mood. I had total destruction more in mind. I rolled over on the bed and clicked through my phone list. I hit the speed dial for Kyla. She picked up almost instantly.

"Hey, what's up? I heard that something happened at the mall," I said.

"Lauren threw this fit in the food court. I mean I love the girl, but sometimes, the drama, you know?"

"So what happened?" I asked.

"Lauren and Justin broke up."

"Really?" I tried to get the right amount of shock in my voice. "So was she really upset? Brokenhearted and all that?"

"Sort of."

"Just sort of? Haven't they gone out forever?"

"Yeah. Maybe that's it. She's bored of him. She seemed more ticked about the fact that he lied to her about something than the fact that they broke up. Lauren doesn't like it when people don't sort of fall in line."

"But still, it's her boyfriend. I would have thought he was super important to her. Shouldn't she be crushed?"

"I don't know, I guess. Maybe she likes someone else."

"Who?"

"Got me. She's never said anything about anyone else, but she also doesn't rave about Justin either. He was more like an accessory, you know?"

"Huh," I muttered. That put a kink in my plan. What was the fun of breaking up Lauren and her boyfriend if she didn't even care? I chewed on the corner of my thumbnail for a second.

"So are you going out with us tonight?"

"I made other plans." I could tell Kyla wanted to ask what other plans, but she didn't want to let on that she was out of the loop on any possible social options at Lincoln High. I was too tired to deal with Lauren's drama and needed the time to come up with how to take the plan to the next stage given this disturbing Justin news. I was just staying home, but if Kyla thought I had better plans, I was willing to let her think it.

"Would you mind if I borrowed your boots through the rest of the weekend? I'll polish them up before I give them back."

"Sure." I said absently while I tried to figure out the next step.

Kyla squealed. "You're the best. I really appreciate it."

"No worries. You know, if you want, you can keep them. Just let me borrow them once in a while," I said.

There was silence on the other line for a second.

"Oh-my-god-are-you-serious? That-is-so-awesome," Kyla said, stringing all her words together. "Anytime you want to borrow them, I mean any time, you just say the word."

"Deal. Look, I gotta run okay?" I said, but Kyla hardly noticed because no doubt she was already plotting new outfits. I punched the phone off and leaned back against the bed.

Getting revenge was more complicated than it had looked blocked out in my binder. In theory everything was going exactly according to plan. Lauren's two best friends were finding themselves more and more annoyed with her. I, the mysterious New York City girl, got way more stealth glances and blatant kiss-up compliments from random peons in the hallway, at least for now. Her status as top of the social heap was starting to erode. She was still up there, but the ground beneath her was unstable. I had known I would never steal her boyfriend out from under her. Justin wasn't the type to actually cheat, he was too all-American, but I had even found a way around that. I didn't have to steal him, I just had to make Lauren think that she might not be the center of his universe. She would never take the chance that he would break up with her. How would that look, after all? No, I knew Lauren would dump him first. And she did, just the way I expected. Well, except for the part where she didn't seem to care. I had expected that to go differently. I didn't necessarily think she would be gutted, but I had hoped for a bigger reaction.

I pulled my binder out from under my bed. I flipped through the pages. I was popular, her friends were starting to like me more than her, Lauren's relationship was over, but it wasn't enough. It wasn't anywhere near enough. I looked at the other two bullet points under Lauren's name. It was time to move on to the next stage of the plan.

Chapter Eighteen

The rest of the evening was frustrating. I made a list of ways to get Lauren off the cheerleading team. It wouldn't be enough if she quit. She had to get kicked off. Unlike the situation with Justin, there needed to be no mistaking the fact that quitting wasn't her choice. It needed that added dimension of humiliation. I made a list of possibilities in my binder:

1. Some type of tragic cheerleading injury due to negligence (Is drunken cheering illegal?)
2. Busted for taking pictures of elementary school kids in compromising positions
3. Doing something very unsportswomanship-like, such as beating up our school mascot
4. Failing all her classes (perhaps declared functionally illiterate) and thus losing her sports eligibility
5. Caught starring in a cheerleaders-gone-wild video

None of the options I came up with seemed very workable. It was going to require more research. I decided to go with just making her life generally miserable until I had a better plan.

Sunday mornings the Wood family could be counted on to go to church no matter the weather. If a once-in-a-century blizzard struck the area, then you could bet Mr. Wood would purchase a dogsled team and mush his family there to prove their commitment to being upstanding members of the community. It wasn't that they were particularly religious—they never prayed over dinner and their house didn't have any Virgin Mary statues planted in the front lawn or anything. If I had to guess, Lauren's favorite saint would be Judas, patron of betrayers. I never heard either of Lauren's parents mention God, unless you counted the times her mom would say, "For the love of God, turn down the TV." Like many things the Wood family did, they went to church because it looked good. It was one more check box on their list proving what an all-American family they were.

To me it didn't matter if they were in church for a true religious calling or if they were faking it. The point was, I could count on all of them being out of the house for at least an hour. I parked a block or two down from their house and waited until I saw their car pull out of the driveway. I got out of my car and walked quickly over to the house and slipped open the gate to the backyard. I stood there waiting. This was the first part of my revenge plan that, if you were going to be technical about things, was illegal.

Lauren's older brother, Josh, had his bedroom on the first

floor. He was off at college, but I was counting on the fact that his window would still be unlocked. Years ago, when Josh was in junior high, he had broken the latch so that it looked locked, but with a good push it would slide right open so he could sneak out and in whenever he wanted. I wandered through the backyard trying to look casual in case any of their neighbors were looking out from their houses. The screen popped right off and I placed it on the ground and gave a quick look around. I yanked on the window. It slid open ridiculously easy; it practically flew off the track. I waited for the sound of sirens, or perhaps a neighbor yelling, but nothing.

One quick jump and a pull, and my front half slipped through the window. Where Josh's bed used to be was now a desk and I slid onto it, knocking a stack of papers to the floor. Shit.

Apparently after Josh went off to college Mrs. Wood had redone his room. I would have thought she was the type of mom to keep her kid's room a shrine to his childhood long after he left, but as it turns out, she was more the type to turn his bedroom into a den. I wonder what Josh thought of the forest green duck theme that was going on. The bookshelf was littered with wooden duck decoys. Their eyes looked a bit desperate to me. I had to fight the urge to stuff them into my bag and release them back into the wild. I picked up the papers on the floor and tried to tell if there had been a specific order. When I couldn't figure it out, I shuffled them back into a tidy pile and hoped no one would notice.

As I slipped through the house, I could see that Mrs. Wood had been busy with redecorating since I had been there last. It seemed to be done in an English country cottage style, heavy on the chintz fabric and overstuffed furniture. Something about the decor made me want to sneeze, as if I were allergic to bad floral design. The staircase wall was a gallery of family photos. There was a giant 14 x 16 of Lauren in her cheerleader outfit near the top. I paused to make the frame hang on a crooked angle. I would have colored in her teeth with a marker, but that might have been a bit too obvious.

Lauren's room was the same Barbie pink it had been when we were kids, but the canopy that had hung over her bed was gone, as were most of the stuffed animals. Most likely she had them put down when she no longer had a use for them. The bedspread was a floral and the furniture was all painted a soft distressed white. The room looked like Laura Ashley had thrown up all over everything. No time to look around. Lauren may not care that much about Justin, but her wardrobe was a different story. I went over to Lauren's closet and pulled out her favorite pair of shoes. I took the left shoe and shoved it into my handbag. I liked the idea of her looking for it, holding the remaining shoe and thinking that the other one had to be there somewhere. I rifled through her hangers, grabbed a few things that I knew she liked, and sat down on the bed. I pulled a seam ripper from my bag and went to work. On one blouse I loosened all the threads that held the right sleeve, I took off three buttons on another. I took the hem out on one of her pant legs. Her jeans took me the most time. I cut every third thread on the seam in the butt.

I shot a look at the clock on her nightstand. Time to get moving: They would be home before too long. I sat down at Lauren's desk and jostled the computer mouse. Her computer was on hibernation mode so it fired right to life. Open on the screen was a paper she was writing for English. On the desk was a copy of Cliff's Notes. *Tsk tsk.* This could count as cheating. I looked around in case anyone was sneaking up on me and then hit delete. One term paper—gone. Consider it a form of academic discipline: If she really wanted to write a paper on the theme of *The Color Purple*, then she should start with reading the book. I rifled through the papers on her desk but didn't see anything that would help me. I opened her desk drawers at random. I crouched down and slid my hand between her mattress and box spring. When we were kids this is where she had kept her Disney Princess locking diary. She had either given up journal writing or had found a more creative hiding place. I looked around for evidence that would give away any secret crushes. If Justin wasn't the love of her life, maybe there was someone else. But the pictures that sat in frames on the dresser were mostly her, Bailey, and Kyla.

I stood in the middle of the room and looked around. What was I missing? I gave the clock another look. Shit, church would be over soon. I reached into my purse and took out the Ziploc bag I had brought. I scooped out the tablespoon of tuna fish inside and dropped it into the heat duct. That should fester after a day or two. I stepped into her bathroom. Lauren appeared to have every possible goo and potion. I picked up her perfume bottle, Clinique Happy. I gave a quick squirt onto my wrists. My hands slid over her things: eye shadow, lip liners, pressed powder, lip sticks, glitter gloss, eye liners, toners, creams, and bronzers. Finally I found it, black mascara. I caught a glimpse of myself in the mirror. I was giving an evil smile that reminded me of Dr. Seuss's Grinch. I pulled a package out of my bag. It was one of those lip-plumping lip glosses. My mom hated those lip glosses and had pointed out to me that they contained capsaicin to make your lips swell. Capsaicin is an extract from chili peppers. I took Lauren's mascara brush out of the tube and swabbed it into the lip-gloss two or three times and then shoved it back into the tube. Victory. Nothing like a little chili pepper to the eye to put a smile on a girl's face.

I took my time leaving the house. I wanted to make sure I didn't leave anything behind, not a speck of dust could be out of place. I peeked out the window before I climbed out, but the coast was clear. The window slid shut, giving a satisfying click as it closed. I did my best to walk slowly back to my car, but it was hard to avoid skipping.

I could hardly wait for Monday.

Chapter Nineteen

$\mathcal{B}$efore school started, the popular kids hung out on the back staircase into the building, provided that the weather was decent. Although there was nothing posted, everyone else knew this area was off-limits unless you were in the upper echelon, in the same way they knew the stoner kids owned the wooded strip at the back of the parking lot where they could smoke weed and pretend no one could see them. Monday morning, I sat next to Bailey and Kyla on the cold cement steps, sipping our Starbucks coffee and talking about our respective weekends. I saw Lauren first; she was walking toward the door from the parking lot, her pace slow.

"Hey, you okay?" Bailey asked, as Lauren drew closer. It was clear Lauren was anything but okay; her eyes were red and swollen. Chili pepper in mascara: one; Lauren Wood: zero.

"I know it's early in the day, but use your brain. Do I look okay?"

Bailey's mouth snapped shut; I could hear her teeth click together.

"I heard about you and Justin. I guess the breakup got to you more than you expected, huh?" I said trying to sound suitably sympathetic. Lauren's mouth pressed together until her lips almost disappeared.

"I haven't been crying. I had some kind of allergic reaction or something." Lauren gave a sniff as if to prove her point.

"Of course you did," Bailey offered. "There can be all kinds of weird pollen and stuff in the fall."

Lauren's nostrils flared and she looked around to see how many people were listening. For once she didn't want to be the center of attention.

"You should get that checked out. Maybe you've got shingles," I suggested.

"Are you saying I've got some kind of disease?"

I placed my hand on my heart as if shocked at her attack. "I didn't mean like a sexually transmitted one or anything. Shingles is like chicken pox. I guess it could also be pink eye."

"Just drop it, okay?" Lauren said, giving her watery eyes another swipe.

"Do you want some of my latte?" Bailey offered.

"Lattes have milk, Bailey. Think about it."

"Sorry."

"Sorry for being stupid or sorry for the latte?" Lauren asked with a snarl.

Bailey's lower lip started to shake and her eyes welled up to match Lauren's.

"Somebody woke up on the wrong side of the bed," a voice behind Lauren said, and we all turned to see who it was.

I hadn't seen him before, and I certainly would have noticed if I had. He was tall and lanky with dark, curly hair. His lower lip was larger than the top and it gave him this sultry pout. His jeans were faded and looked as if they would be as soft as flannel to the touch—and oh, I wanted to touch.

"Bailey knows I'm just joking," Lauren said with a toss of her hair, her voice suddenly light and playful.

He looked over at Bailey who was still staring at her shoes. "Quite the sense of humor you got there," he said to Lauren.

I gave a tiny snort that I instantly tried to turn into a cough.

"Don't be mean. You should know me by now." Lauren cocked her hip at an angle. "I'm a tease."

"That's what I hear," said the mystery boy.

Bailey looked up at him with a smile and he gave her a wink. He looked closer at Lauren and then pulled back.

"Looks like you need to lay off the heavy drinking," he said, motioning to her eyes.

"It's an allergic reaction to something."

"Hope it clears up before tryouts next week. Nobody likes an Eliza Doolittle who looks like a crack addict."

"It'll clear up. What's this I hear—you'll be filming the whole thing?" Lauren asked.

"It's for an independent study. I'm doing a documentary."

"Cool," I said.

He gave a shrug and started to move up the stairs. He looked over at me and then looked down at my chest. The corner of his mouth turned up into a slight smile.

"Nice shirt," he said, lifting his gaze to meet my eyes.

With him looking at me like that I couldn't recall what I was wearing. I was too involved in a fantasy where the two of us were wearing far less. I glanced down at my shirt. It was a T-shirt with a print of the 1949 *Wizard of Oz* movie poster. I looked at Judy Garland's face and tried to think of something smart to say.

"Thanks," I mumbled.

"So which character are you?"

"Dorothy, I guess. Strange girl in a strange place."

He looked at me carefully, cocking his head from one side to the other. "No, Dorothy doesn't suit you. I think you might be more complex. I'm thinking lion—bluff and bluster, but a softie inside. See you around Oz, Lion Girl," he said, moving past us and walking up the stairs. I watched him until he went through the doors.

"Who was that?" I asked, spinning back around.

"Christopher Morgan," Kyla said. "Lincoln High's official rebel without a cause."

"Don't bother. He never dates anyone here," Lauren said. "He's totally focused on his art. Unlike other people around here, he's a real artist."

"What makes you think I want to date him?"

"Apart from the fact your tongue was hanging out when you talked to him?" Lauren sniffed. "Anyway, Chris is going to be a serious filmmaker."

"He's nice," Bailey offered.

"You think everyone's nice," Lauren grumped, plunking down on the stairs next to Kyla. Lauren looked over at Bailey who had gone back to staring at her shoes and chewing on her lower lip. "Don't be ticked at me, I'm having a lousy morning. The whole day was craptacular before the thing with my eyes started. I got completely dressed and then I couldn't find my other shoe so I had to change outfits. Then my new shirt was missing a button. So I had to change all over again. The whole thing was a nightmare. Besides, you know me, I just say stuff."

"I'm not stupid," Bailey said.

Lauren rolled her eyes at Kyla. "Of course you're not stupid." The first morning bell rang and everyone around us started to move toward the doors. "I'm going to run to the bathroom and try to do something with my face." Lauren stood and gathered up her things.

"I'll meet you guys in French," Kyla said, moving up the stairs. "I have to drop off my brother's medication with the nurse first."

Bailey gave a slight wave to Kyla. I stayed in place to watch Lauren walk away. The seat of her jeans was split all down the center seam, and as she moved up the stairs, you could see a wink of her bright pink thong and plenty of white Lauren butt cheek. Bailey's eyes grew wide.

"Lauren!" Bailey cried out. Lauren turned around and I grabbed Bailey's arm, giving it a squeeze. She looked over at me, her eyebrows crinkling together in confusion.

"What?" Lauren placed a hand on one hip.

"Nothing. We just wanted to say we'll save you a place at lunch," I said.

"Okay, whatever." Lauren gave her hair another toss and bounced up the stairs, pink and white flashing in the gap in the back of her pants. Bailey waited until she was gone and then looked at me for an explanation.

"She must know it's there. After all, someone would have to be stupid not to know there was a huge hole in her pants," I said, keeping my face serious. I could see the wheels turning behind Bailey's eyes.

This was a calculated risk on my part. Bailey was most likely the nicest person alive. With her long blond hair, blue eyes, and Mary Poppins approach to the world it was possible she would think I was a vile person to let Lauren be embarrassed. She could race after Lauren and stop her from going any farther. She could even let Lauren in on the fact that I had been willing to let her flash the entire school. On the other hand, maybe, just maybe, part of her was sick of Lauren's crap too. Was it possible that Lauren could drive even Mary Poppins to being a conspirator to my evil deed?

Bailey's lips quivered and a shy smile snuck out. She glanced at me and then away. She looked back and had a huge smile on her face.

"Come on, we should get to French," she said, linking arms with me.

"Why, I would be delighted to attend French with you," I said, giving her a warm smile back. We marched down the hall in tandem. It said a lot about Lauren that she could make a Mary Poppins clone want to do her harm.

"Now tell me more about this Christopher fellow," I said. "Just how nice is he?"

Chapter Twenty

Brenda practically danced into biology class; her new look clearly agreed with her. Her hair looked great and she was wearing one of her new outfits—slim black pants, ballet flats, and the white shirt starched stiff. She was even walking less Lurchlike. She looked surprised to see me sitting at her lab table. She raised an eyebrow in question and slowed her pace.

"I asked Melvin to change with me," I explained. "You don't mind having me as a lab partner, do you?"

"I don't know. Melvin's a whiz with a Bunsen burner. Besides, people will see us together. Will your reputation survive?"

I didn't say anything and instead passed her a pencil drawing I had done over the weekend.

"It's Einstein," I said in case she didn't recognize him. Brenda took the picture and looked it over.

"Thanks. You're really good."

I shrugged. I never knew what to say when people complimented me on my art. I was just glad that Brenda wasn't going to demand that I change back with Melvin. I liked her despite myself, and if we were lab partners, we had a great reason to hang out, all without blowing my reputation. With her makeover she looked pretty decent. Besides, there is a long and glorious tradition of popular people being friendly with the smart types when there are grades on the line.

"Nice hair," a girl said as she walked past our table to the supply closet. Brenda blushed and mumbled her thanks.

"I take it the new look has been a hit." I crossed my arms. "Guess maybe I was onto something with the idea that looks matter."

Brenda shrugged. She turned away from me to pull her things out of her bag, but I could see a hint of a smile on her face. "I'm not sure it's exactly earth-shattering news to admit that people are obsessed with appearances."

"No, the earth-shattering part is that you're paying attention."

"It's an experiment."

"Anything for science."

Mr. Wong, our biology teacher, rapped on his desk to get our attention. He had a project for the class. He was sending us out to collect swabs from different surfaces in the school so we could discover just how much bacteria was thriving in the building. We were to write up our expectations and then let the swab gunk grow in some petri dishes for a couple weeks to see what came up. Who says science can't be fun?

Brenda considered where to collect our swabs with great care. She had a future as a health department inspector if she wanted; she took her bacteria very seriously.

"I'm thinking we should do some from the bathroom and then some from the cafeteria tables. The assumption would be that the bathroom would have more bacteria, but my money is on the cafeteria. Have you ever seen them wash down the tables? They use the same nasty rag and a bucket that I am sure is an open sewer of disease." She chewed her lip, thinking things over.

"Mmm, nothing makes me hungrier than talk of sewers and bacteria," I said. We walked down toward the cafeteria. I had an idea. "We should collect a swab from the girl's bathroom and another one from the guy's along with the cafeteria."

"That's a good idea." Brenda looked over at me, surprised.

"What? Just because I look good doesn't mean I don't have a brain." I gave a disgusted snort. "And here you act upset about people judging people by their looks. Pot, kettle, black," I said with a singsong voice.

Getting the swabs from the girl's bathroom and the cafeteria was easy. With those secured Brenda and I stood outside the boy's bathroom.

"Maybe you should go in and get it," Brenda suggested. "I'll stand out here and make sure no one goes in."

"You're the scientist, shouldn't you go? It will be like field-work. You can be the Jane Goodall of the men's room." We both peered up and down the hall. "Look, I'll do it, but you're coming with me. We don't have all day." I shoved open the door and pulled Brenda in behind me by her wrist.

"It doesn't look that different," she said with surprise.

"What you were thinking? Wood paneling, maybe some animal heads mounted on the wall?"

Brenda walked over to the stall wall and started looking over the varied things scribbled on it. Her nose wrinkled up. "This is disgusting."

"Yep. The bathroom wall, where poets leave their finest work. It's amazing how many words rhyme with fart." I surveyed the space. "Where do you want to get the swab from?"

"Floor by the toilet. It should be the same as the girl's room. That way we can use it as a comparison."

"Fair enough. I'll swab, you stand by the door and hum or something so no one wanders in."

I pushed the stall door open and gave a quick look behind me. Brenda was by the door. I whipped out a Sharpie and wrote quickly on the wall: LAUREN WOOD PUTS OUT. Then I paused. Would that be considered a bonus? Would it have been better to put down LAUREN WOOD IS FRIGID? What would she see as the ultimate insult? Then it came to me. I added, BUT WHO CARES?

As I bent to get the sample, Brenda started singing in an effort to scare off any rogue bathroom users. Her voice was clear and strong as it bounced off the tile walls. I stopped thinking about Lauren, revenge, or biology swabs. I backed up so I could see her. She was leaning against the sink as if her singing was no big deal. She was singing a song I didn't know. It sounded sort of sad and mournful, but something about her voice made you feel like things would be okay. She turned around and noticed me staring at her.

"What?"

"What are you doing?"

"You told me to sing." Brenda's face flushed red. There was no way she was ever going to go into a life of crime; she looked guilty when she hadn't even done anything.

"That was amazing. What was it?"

"It's an Irish folk song."

"You're really good."

"I sing at my church. I've been in the choir for a few years."

I waved my hand dismissively. "Skip church. You should be singing on the radio. You could be on *American Idol* or something."

Brenda raised one eyebrow.

"Okay, maybe *American Idol* isn't your style, but I'm serious. You're really good," I said.

"Thanks. Why do you look so surprised?"

"I don't know. It's just unexpected. If you had memorized the entire periodic table it would be amazing, but not that surprising. You're a woman of mystery, no doubt about it."

"Did you get the sample?"

I held up the swab and Brenda clicked the plastic top over the tip, preserving our carefully gathered bacteria. She fanned out the three swabs in her hand and looked at them closely as if she could see the microscopic creatures already breeding on the tips. She looked satisfied with a job well done.

"Once we get a good look at them through the microscope we should do up some graphics. You're the art guru—you can make up some color sketches."

"Well, with all this extra credit fun I can see Melvin is going to be upset you're not his lab partner anymore."

Brenda smirked and yanked open the bathroom door, heading back to Wong's class. The idea came to me in a flash; it was so perfect, it took my breath away.

The door closed behind Brenda, and I stood there looking at it, while taking short, shallow breaths. The door opened back up and Brenda peeked her head in.

"So, you coming or are you planning to stay here?"

I stepped out after her into the hallway.

"Brenda?" She turned to look at me. "Have you ever considered trying out for the school play? With a voice like yours, you could take the lead."

Chapter Twenty-One

$\mathcal{L}$auren wasn't at lunch. Apparently she made it to third period before anyone told her about her pants. To me this proved that I wasn't the only one who couldn't stand her. Lauren had gone home to change. Kyla started laughing when she told the story, and then we all agreed that of course it wasn't really funny. We were simply laughing with her, not at her.

I left lunch early so I could find Ms. Herbaut, the drama teacher. Rumor was that Ms. Herbaut had been on the verge of fame and glory on the stage when she gave it all up to move to middle-of-nowhere Michigan to marry her one true love. Although this story had a lovely romance novel–like quality, I was more skeptical. My hunch was that Ms. Herbaut got sick of living in a dumpy studio apartment, waiting tables, and hustling to audition after audition, where, if she was lucky, she would end up earning the role of "peasant number two" in an off-Broadway production of Shakespeare.

Ms. Herbaut's room was near the auditorium, and she'd decorated the walls with various playbills and those annoying kitty just-hang-in-there type posters. I wonder if adults really think we're going to get to the end of our ropes, ready to hurl ourselves off a bridge somewhere, and the sight of a cute kitty will turn us around. Saved by big-eyed kittens. Speaking for myself, I don't want to settle for just hanging in there.

Ms. Herbaut wasn't in the room even though this was supposed to be her assigned office hour. I wandered around, stopping at the giant bulletin board at the back. She had pinned up pictures from the film version of *My Fair Lady* and slips of paper with the song lyrics. In the center of the board there was information about the upcoming auditions. I pulled a scrap of paper out of my bag and made a few notes. Brenda still wasn't sold on the idea, but I was working on her.

"So, Lion, we meet again. What has you so far off the yellow brick road?"

I spun around and Christopher, the good-looking guy from this morning, was leaning against the doorjamb. I felt my tongue dry out and I swallowed deeply.

"I'm Claire."

"Cowardly Claire?"

"Courageous," I shot back. He gave a half smile and my stomach fell into a free fall to the floor.

"What makes someone move from New York to this neck of the woods?"

"How do you know I'm from New York?"

"I asked about you." He took another step closer, and I felt my heart pick up its pace. It was slamming around in my chest like I was sprinting uphill.

"What else did you find out?"

"Not much." Christopher motioned to the bulletin board. "You planning to try out for the play?"

"I'm more of a behind-the-scenes person. I was going to check with Ms. Herbaut to see if I could volunteer to stage-manage or something."

"Ah, you like to be the power behind the throne, huh?"

I gave a high and squeaky laugh that made me sound like I'd been sucking helium. I cleared my throat and tried to say something smart. "I hear you're a filmmaker. I wouldn't think you'd want to be involved with a school play."

"So you've been asking about me too?" His smile grew wider. "I'm going to do a documentary short on the play, a sort of drama-behind-the-drama kind of thing. I want to be a director."

"You like Hitchcock?" I asked, hoping that he wouldn't say something like "Hitchcock who?"

Christopher's face lit up. "I love Hitchcock. The man was a master. *Strangers on a Train*? Brilliant."

"I love the costumes in those black-and-white films."

"Old movies are boring," said a voice behind us, and we both turned around. It was Lauren, wearing a new pair of jeans.

She walked over and stood close to Christopher. She looked at me with her nose scrunched up. Her eyes were better, the puffiness was gone, but they were still red.

"What do you think?" Christopher asked me. "Do you have a Hitchcock favorite?"

"*Vertigo*. Hands down. Didn't do well when it was released, but no doubt about it, it's one of his best."

Christopher gave a slight appreciative nod. "Some critics call it one of the best movies ever."

"Did you know they only had like sixteen days of on-site filming?"

"That's cool—I didn't know that." Christopher gave me an appraising look.

"More than just a pretty face," I said.

Christopher opened his mouth to say something, but Lauren cut him off. "So, I thought you said you weren't trying out for the play." Her face was still squished up as if she smelled something bad. She took a slight step forward as if she were trying to use her body to create a wall between the two of us.

"You made it sound like so much fun, I decided to see if I could help out," I said.

"Oh." Lauren greeted the news that I would be involved with the play with the same level of excitement that others use to greet news of impending dental work. Her nostrils were flaring in and out. Mr. Ed grows annoyed.

"So you like old movies, huh?" Lauren's eyes narrowed.

Uh-oh. Helen loved old movies. Claire was supposed to be a completely different person. Showing off for Christopher was going to cost me.

"No. I mean, well, yeah. I mean, I just like movies in general. An ex-boyfriend of mine was in film school in New York. I could take it or leave it."

"Oh," Christopher said, sounding disappointed. "Here I thought I found a kindred spirit."

I shrugged, wishing I could throw myself under a bus. "Sorry."

"Well, Lion, I'll see you around then." Christopher gave Lauren a quick smile and shuffled toward the door. He didn't simply walk, he moseyed.

"Are you headed to gym?" Lauren called after him. Christopher nodded. "I'll walk with you. I was going to ask Ms. H. a question, but I bet you can help me."

Lauren was looking up at Christopher, and I could see it in her face. She was crazy about him. Over-the-moon crazy. Disney singing wildlife, *fa-la-la-la* kind of crazy. Christopher was everything that Lauren's mother would hate—family from the wrong side of the tracks, earring, too-long hair, career plans that didn't involve wearing a suit and earning obscene amounts of money. Even though they were opposites, it was clear from the way she looked at him she was head over heels. No wonder she wasn't that sorry about Justin. Maybe she thought it was time to throw caution, and herself, to the wind . . . and at Christopher.

Doing my best to woo Christopher away from her grasp wasn't even going to feel like work. This wasn't revenge; it was a public service. No one that good should be with someone so bad.

Chapter Twenty-Two

Grandma looked at the half-cooked carcass. She gave it a poke with her fork. "Do you think those onions are caramelizing? They don't look caramel to me. They look soggy."

I peered at the chicken that was squatting on a bed of sliced lemons, fennel, and onions. She didn't really need my opinion; she could make a gourmet meal out of nothing but a soft carrot from the bottom of the crisper drawer, a slice of toast, and the spices no one ever uses, like coriander seed.

"I think the recipe called for too much broth. The onions are just boiling in there, practically floating." She shook her head at the tragedy.

I gave a sigh. Chicken advice I didn't need.

She looked at me. "Sorry about that. Tell me the problem again."

"My friend Brenda doesn't want to try out for the play."

"Maybe the play isn't her kind of thing."

"It's not. She's not good at the spotlight. She's more of a books and laboratories kind of person."

"Well, then there you go." Grandma drained some of the broth and chicken fat into the sink. "So if she doesn't want to do it, why does that frost your cookies? Just because you're doing the play doesn't mean she has to do it with you. Friends can have different interests."

I rolled my eyes. Grandma was usually pretty good at this, but every so often, usually if she had been watching too much *Dr. Phil,* her advice got all cheesy. Of course, I couldn't tell her the real reason I needed Brenda to try out for the play. Grandma was out of the revenge loop.

"It's not that. I can do the play on my own. It's that I think she would be really good. It seems like a waste to have all that talent and then not use it."

"Not like you and art."

I sighed again. Grandma was on my case to pull together some kind of portfolio so I could apply to college art programs. It wasn't that I didn't like to draw, but I hated the idea of sticking my stuff in between plastic sheets so everyone could *ooh* and *aah* and decide if it was any good. I wasn't even sure I wanted to go to college, which was fine with my parents who are all about "finding yourself," but Grandma is all about the value of a college education.

Grandma had always been the sane one in my family. She stayed in the same house versus moving from apartment to apartment. She remembered to pay her property taxes, and you would never catch her out in the backyard naked at midnight chanting at the moon. I loved that her linen closet was full of towels and sheets as opposed to ours, which was always full of plants and herbs my mom was drying out. I used to love to visit my grandma's because it seemed like what a home was supposed to be, but now that we were living together, I was discovering the downside. Grandma believed in regular mealtimes and lights out by eleven. My parents never gave me a curfew because they felt that to learn responsibility I had to have freedom. Grandma was more of the "be home by midnight, Cinderella, or turn into a pumpkin" kind of guardian. She wasn't keen on the whole "letting life unfold" thing. She wanted me to have a plan for my future. She was becoming borderline annoying about the whole art school thing.

"You can't talk someone into something they don't want to do," Grandma said. "All you can do is point out what you think is in it for them. Not why you think they should do it, but what might appeal to them." She brushed her hair out of her eyes and I laughed. "What's so funny?"

Her hands must have had grease from the chicken on them because her hair now looked like she last took a shower in the early summer. I pointed at her head and she reached up, giving a curse when she felt the oil.

A flash of inspiration came to me. I stuck the chicken back in the oven for her while she went to wash up and hummed a victory tune. Grandma was still helping me with my revenge plan, even if she didn't know it.

Chapter Twenty-Three

*B*renda cared for our bacteria with a love and affection that some people don't show their flesh-and-blood children. She would sneak in between classes to coo encouragingly at them, cheering on their growth. We had swiped two petri dishes per swab, and one of our dishes that had been swabbed from the girl's bathroom had died after only two days. It wasn't clear what had happened, but Brenda was devastated. She worried that it would throw off our entire paper. I pointed out that we weren't trying to find a cure for cancer and that it is somewhat unnatural to be that upset over dead bacteria. I wouldn't have been surprised to find out she had a small ceremony for them before she dumped the petri dish in the garbage.

A week after collecting the samples, we were at Brenda's, working on our paper. Brenda sat at her computer, her face set in a serious expression. She was looking through the rough sketches I had done for our project. I was lying on her floor, in theory studying for our test, but there is only so much information I can absorb about the life span of bacteria and viruses. In my mind I replayed the day's victory. While Lauren had been in gym class, I went to the locker room and poured olive oil into her hair spray. Knowing her affinity for excessive product use, I had not been surprised to discover that her hair ended up with so much oil that it basically repelled water. It hung from her head in greasy clumps. She tried to wash it out, but she couldn't get it all. As a result she had to go through the rest of the afternoon looking vaguely homeless and smelling like an Italian restaurant.

"I don't think the color is quite right," Brenda mumbled, breaking into my happy flashback. She was holding the picture close and then far away. "I think they look too pink."

I rolled up into a sitting position and scooted over toward her desk.

"What's wrong? Those are lovely bacteria. Did you see what I did with their tails? Very chic."

"Tails?" Brenda raised an eyebrow. "Flagella would be the term you're looking for."

"Right." I watched Brenda as she scrolled the mouse over the computer screen looking at the various shades of pink available in the color wheel and holding up the drawing to compare. She leaned back to get a better view. "You really like this stuff, don't you?" I said.

"What, science?"

"Yeah. Who else cares what color pink their bacteria end up being?"

"What's strange about liking science? I like knowing how things work," she said.

"I can totally see you being a CSI, working in a swanky glass lab down in Miami."

"That show is total bunk, you know. They make it look like you can run a DNA sample in the time it takes to do a Google search."

"What? TV lies? Tell me it isn't true!" I threw my hands up in the air.

"Ha ha. I don't want to be a CSI, even if it means a fancy lab."

"So what are you going to do with all this science know-how?"

"I want to be an astronaut," she said with a solemn voice.

I started to laugh and then realized she wasn't joking.

"Serious? You want to be a space ranger?"

"I was thinking more something with NASA but, yeah, I'm serious."

"When you go to Mars will you paint my name on a rock up there or something? Maybe bring me back some kind of tiny alien I could keep in an aquarium on my desk?"

"I'm pretty sure NASA frowns on those kind of things, but I'll see what I can do. What about you?"

"I could never be an astronaut. I throw up on roller coasters, and I'm pretty sure being shot into space is more traumatic than that."

"I was being serious," Brenda said.

"So am I. When I was nine, my dad took me to Six Flags. I sprayed down a group of Korean tourists with half-digested Fruit Loops and soy milk. Trust me, those Koreans will always remember their American experience. I bet they never got the smell out."

"I meant, what do you want to do for a living?"

"I don't know," I said with a shrug.

"You're really good at art. You could do graphics or something."

"Mmm, the thrill of designing ads for feminine products, much more meaningful than your shallow goal of exploring space for humanity."

Brenda rolled her eyes and turned back to her computer. She chewed on the end of her pencil.

That was it! Grandma's advice to the rescue again. Suddenly I knew my angle. "You know, I bet it's hard to be an astronaut. I suspect NASA only takes candidates from the best schools and stuff, huh?" I asked.

"Well, it's not like they recruit from the vocational programs if that's what you're asking."

"Yeah, come to think of it, you never see any job postings for astronauts in the classified ads. No wonder you worry so much about your grades."

Brenda looked over at me. "What's your point?"

"I'm just thinking you want to make sure your college apps are killer. Give yourself the best chance to get into the best schools."

"Uh-huh."

"Important to be well-rounded though too. They look at more than just grades, you know." I shook my head knowingly.

Brenda pulled her chair back with a yank. "Not again."

"What?"

"You're bringing up the school play thing."

I snapped my fingers as if the connection just came to me. "That's brilliant! Being in the school play is exactly the kind of thing that can round out an application. Gives you an edge—shows you've got the artsy side and the science side."

"Why do you want me to do this so badly?" Brenda asked. "What does it matter to you?"

"You're amazing. You shouldn't keep that kind of talent to yourself. It's, like, criminal. Besides, it would be good for you."

"Like eating broccoli."

"No, like pushing yourself to try new things. Admit it, you like to sing, right?" I asked.

"Yeah, but I don't like being up in front of huge crowds of people, I don't like being the center of attention, and when you round those things out with the fact that I haven't done a single play in my entire life, it seems like maybe going out for the show isn't the best plan ever."

"That's the very reason that you should do it."

"How do you figure?"

"You think NASA wants astronauts who shy away from a challenge?" I pushed.

Brenda tapped her pencil and looked out the window.

"I wouldn't know how to go about trying out even if I wanted to," she admitted.

I scooched up closer. We had moved from no to logistics.

"You sing one song—I'd recommend something that shows your range—and then you do a short monologue. I can help you pick one out and practice."

Brenda's foot bounced up and down as she thought it over.

"You would help me learn the monologue?"

"Totally. Look at it this way: Worst case scenario, you don't get a part. You don't have a part now so, really, no big loss."

"Except for the part where I could make a total ass of myself."

"No guts, no glory." I waited a few beats. "Captain Kirk would go for it."

Brenda shot me a look. "Captain Kirk?"

"I can't remember the name of the woman captain. Star Trek isn't really my thing."

"Captain Janeway," Brenda said.

"There you go. Janeway would try out for the play."

"What about you?"

"What about me?"

"What can I help you do, if you're going to help me with this? What is it you want to do?"

"I'm really not holding out on you. I don't know what I want." I picked at the carpet. There was no way to explain that what I wanted was to make Lauren's life miserable. More than miserable. I wanted her to think miserable would be a step up from where her life had sunk. I needed her to lose everything that mattered to her: her boyfriend, her friends, her popularity. She sold me out to get those things and I planned to take them back. I hadn't really considered what I would do after that. It almost felt like if I had another goal, the universe would decide I was too greedy and not give me either thing I wanted.

"You must have some idea of what you want to do with your life long-term."

"Not really."

"So what are you going to do after graduation?" Brenda sounded shocked.

"I figure I'll sort it out when I get to college." I could see her eyes widen. "What, a lot of people don't know what they want to do. College is meant to be a time of self-discovery and all that. Don't you read the college catalogs?"

"Okay, forget it."

"If you want to help me, you can help me pass biology."

"Deal." Brenda held out her hand to shake on it.

"So you'll try out for the play?"

"Yes, I'll try out."

I jumped up and pumped my fists into the air. "Yes! Enough coloring cytoplasm. Let's figure out a song for you to sing. Then we can go online and find a good monologue, nothing too over the top. If you ask me, that's where people go wrong. They get too dramatic. Understated will win them over every time."

"Hey," Brenda said, and I stopped pacing and planning to look at her. "I really appreciate this. You're a good friend." She gave me a warm smile.

And just like that, I went from feeling great to feeling like shit.

Chapter Twenty-Four

I started babysitting in seventh grade. Our next-door neighbor back then was Mrs. Kile. She had a son, Jordon, who was four. That kid was equal parts smart and destructive. He took their TV apart and blew the power grid for our whole neighborhood when he stuck something, no one knew what, into the power socket. It was clear that Jordon couldn't be without constant supervision.

It started with his mom calling me to come over when she needed to get something done. I would hang out in their living room and keep Jordon from accidentally building a thermonuclear device using LEGOs and Pop Rocks. The Kiles always had Doritos or string cheese or those plastic pudding cups. I would have done it for the trans-fat snacks alone, but Mrs. Kile insisted on paying me. It was the first money I ever made on my own, unless you count my allowance, which I didn't because it was so small.

There isn't much to do in the summer in Terrace. If I made the mistake of complaining to my parents about being bored they would sign me up for some cheesy day camp and I'd spend the rest of the summer making "art" from nontoxic glue, yarn, and Popsicle sticks. Instead, I would head over to Lauren's and we would hang out at the mall all day. The mall was air conditioned, frequently contained packs of other preteen kids, and had a food court. It was as close as we were going to get to an amusement park. We would go into the stores and talk in loud voices about how we had a very important party to go to and then try on the fancy cocktail dresses. The salesclerks hated us. Once we had tried everything on and eaten at least $10 worth of Dairy Queen we would go to Hudson's Department Store and hang around the makeup counter.

Lauren had strong feelings about makeup. Her mom wore only Chanel cosmetics. She had lotions that were made from ground Peruvian berries, cost more than a small used car, and in theory would stop her aging. My mom, when she wore makeup at all, leaned toward some weird organic brand she bought at the health food store.

"This is the kind of lip gloss I want to get," Lauren said one day the summer before her betrayal. She smoothed on a thin coat from the sample container on the display. The salesclerk, who wore a white coat like she was a doctor working in a research lab, not a peddler of eye shadow, didn't even bother to help us. She leaned against the counter chewing her gum and talking about her boyfriend to the perfume salesclerk across the aisle.

"It looks nice," I said.

"It's not just 'nice.' This lip gloss is made in Paris. Everyone knows that the French do the best lipstick."

"They do?"

"Duh? Why do you think they call it French kissing?"

I wasn't sure she was right, but I also wasn't sure she was wrong. I took the tube from her and inspected it. I put a small bit on my pinky finger and smeared it across my lips just like Lauren had.

"How does it look on me?"

"Good. Try a darker color too." Lauren pulled another sample off the display and passed it over to me. "My mom says that she won't get it for me because she's afraid I'll lose it. As if."

I didn't say anything, but Lauren's mom was right. Lauren was the only person I knew who traveled with her own personal black hole. She was always losing stuff.

I looked at the darker lip gloss on my face. It wasn't me at all. Plus my mom would freak out if she saw me in it. She didn't feel I should wear makeup at all until at least ninth grade.

"I think I'll get a tube of lighter stuff," I said, reaching for the display.

"That stuff costs $25 a tube," Lauren said, her tone pointing out that this type of lip gloss was far from the three-for-the-price-of-two sales at Walgreens.

"It's okay, I've got the money." I pulled my babysitting cash out of my pocket. It lay on the counter sort of crumpled and damp-looking. Lauren looked at me and then down at the money. "I started babysitting for Ms. Kile," I added, my chin thrusting up in a proud way.

"You really should get the darker shade. It goes better with your hair color."

"I like the lighter one better."

"Fine." Lauren turned away with her arms crossed.

"What's the matter?"

"Nothing."

I wasn't sure exactly what was wrong, but I was sure something was. Lauren has a PhD in pouting. No one pouts like her. She could teach lessons to toddlers.

"Are you mad I'm getting the lip gloss?"

"I just think it's rude that you would get the color you know I want."

"But you said your mom wouldn't get it for you."

"Well, that's what she says now, but I would have talked her into it. She would have gotten it for me. Or I would have bought it myself."

"You could get it too. What's wrong with us having the same color?"

"Duh, Helen. If you don't understand, then I don't know how to explain it to you."

"Forget it. I won't get the lip gloss," I said.

"No, go ahead. You want it. It doesn't matter that I wanted it first, so just go ahead and do what you want."

"No, I don't want it anymore. I'll get something else." I hated when Lauren was mad at me. It would ruin the whole day. If she was really ticked, the cold shoulder could last all week. I jammed the money back in my pocket.

"No. Get it." Lauren grabbed a tube of gloss from the display and practically tossed it at the salesclerk. "My friend wants to get this."

"No I don't."

"Yes she does."

Now in addition to Lauren being annoyed with me, the salesclerk was too. "Do you want it or not?" the clerk asked, no doubt already counting down the minutes until summer ended and packs of kids stopped trolling the mall.

"We could share it," I offered. "I can pay for it now, and then we can both use it."

Lauren stopped and turned around so she was facing me. There was a hint of a thaw on her face.

"You would share it with me?"

"Of course. What are best friends for?"

Lauren gave a happy squeak. The clerk did her best to avoid rolling her eyes and wrapped up the tube in tissue before placing it in a tiny glossy shopping bag with the logo of the makeup company in thick, raised gold foil.

"I'll carry it," Lauren said, grabbing the bag as if she were doing me a favor by carrying such a heavy item. We went straight to the ladies' room and each applied a coat of the lip gloss and looked at each other very carefully in the mirror. Once we decided we were suitably fabulous we went back out into the mall. Lauren had a new bounce to her step, and she swung the bag to make sure it attracted the maximum amount of attention.

"It might be better if we kept the lip gloss at my place," Lauren said.

"Why?"

"You know how your mom is. If she sees it she'll have a fit. She'll think you should have sent the money to some group that is saving whales or something stupid like that."

"It's not like I would tell her how much I spent on it. Besides, she pretty much stays out of my stuff."

"Yeah, but whenever we go somewhere we almost always get ready at my place, so if the lip gloss is there, then we'll have it. Otherwise you could forget."

And just like that, it went from my lip gloss to hers. I was like a dad after a divorce with limited visitation rights. Of course the whole thing didn't matter much since about three weeks later Lauren lost the tube of lip gloss altogether. She didn't care as much. She had started babysitting too by that time and was earning her own money. She bought another tube, but there was never any discussion of us sharing it. Later, after the whole "incident," I realized that Lauren did stuff like this all the time.

Turned situations around until I ended up apologizing for nothing at all and she ended up with whatever she wanted in the first place. At the time I had thought Lauren was just more sensitive than me, someone who needed to be treated carefully. Later I realized that she manipulated me and used me all along.

The situation with Brenda was completely different. I wasn't using her. Okay, I was using her a bit, but it wasn't like I was using her to get something for myself. She was being used to get justice, for the greater good. Besides, being in the play was going to benefit Brenda in the long-term. In some ways you could see it as me helping her, encouraging her to be all she can be and that kind of thing.

I lay in bed looking up at the ceiling. I wasn't like Lauren. This situation was nothing like the stuff she used to do to me, the stuff she still pulled with Bailey and Kyla.

Even if it was a less-than-ideal situation, there wasn't a choice. I hadn't come this far to settle for merely giving Lauren greasy hair and torn jeans. It was time for her to pay.

Chapter Twenty-Five

Bailey, Kyla, and I took Lauren out for dinner the night before auditions for good luck. Why we picked dinner was a mystery, as the list of things Lauren wouldn't eat was a mile long. She had to avoid anything that might impact her voice or—God forbid—result in her looking bloated on the big day. It was clear she was nervous.

Unlike Lauren, I was really looking forward to the auditions. I couldn't wait to see her face when Brenda started singing. I was going to have to fight the urge to break into song myself. "*Ding-dong*, the witch is dead . . ." Then there was the added bonus that I would have a chance to talk to Christopher again. I tried to keep the focus on getting closer to Christopher as a means of making sure he didn't fall under Lauren's spell. However, I was willing to admit that the idea of spending time with him was the best part of the revenge plan so far.

Lauren sat there picking at a salad that had anything that

might be considered tasty left off. It appeared to be nothing more than iceberg lettuce with lemon juice on top. I took a big bite of my cheeseburger and tossed it back with a slurp from my milkshake. Lauren glanced at me, disgusted. It was becoming clear that Lauren didn't know quite what to do with me. Due to my nonstop scheming and strategic butt kissing, both Bailey and Kyla loved me. Everyone at school thought I was cosmopolitan and cool. Freshman girls copied how I wore my hair. Lauren was stuck with me. I was like a flea on her otherwise perfectly groomed lapdogs.

"So what does your voice coach say about the audition?" Kyla asked, sticking to safe topics, which included anything focused on Lauren.

"She thinks I'm ready. We've practiced the song since last spring." Lauren stabbed another piece of lettuce. I noticed that the skin around her fingernails was ragged, like she had stuck them in a garbage disposal. Plus, despite a heavy smear of concealer, I could see a flock of small red pimples clustered around her forehead. It looked like my daily sabotages were starting to get to her. I took another satisfied slurp on my milkshake.

"You're going to be great," Bailey said.

"Grrrrrrreat!" I roared in a Tony the Tiger voice. Lauren's eyes narrowed. Bailey and Kyla laughed.

"All I can say is nothing better go wrong," Lauren said, tossing her fork down on her plate to indicate that the five calories she'd consumed had rendered her full.

"Nothing will go wrong," Bailey soothed.

"What could go wrong?" I asked.

"Lately, everything is going wrong."

"Everyone has their ups and downs," I said, as I dragged another fry through my river of ketchup.

"I don't."

That pretty much killed the conversation for a few minutes until Bailey resurrected the thrill-a-minute discussion of how great Lauren's hair looked. I managed to refrain from pointing out that the olive oil had perhaps done some good.

Bailey excused herself to go to the bathroom and Kyla tagged along, leaving Lauren and me sitting across from each other in the booth.

"I don't know what your story is, but I don't trust you," Lauren said.

"What are you talking about?" I managed to meet her eyes, but just barely. After years backing down from Lauren, it was ingrained.

"Ever since you started school here, I've had nothing but bad luck."

"What, you think I have it out for you? Why?" I tried to sound casual, but there was a part of me that almost hoped everything would come to a head, that she would realize who I was and realize just what she had done. I felt a slick of sweat sprout up in my armpits.

Lauren looked around the restaurant, her nostrils flaring

in and out. She really needed to do something about that facial tic.

"This is my senior year and I worked really hard to be where I am," Lauren said, as if that explained anything.

"It's my senior year too. Come to think of it, it's also Bailey's and Kyla's and, oh, give or take a few hundred other people's senior year."

"Whatever." Lauren managed to avoid saying out loud what I was sure she was thinking, which was that our hopes and dreams for our senior year paled in comparison to her own.

"I'm sorry that you don't like me, but for what it's worth, I hope you get the senior year that you deserve," I said with a smile on my face. I popped another fry dripping bloodred ketchup into my mouth.

Chapter Twenty-Six

Auditions were held in the school auditorium. I sat with a clipboard and my grandma's cat's-eye reading glasses, trying to look official. I was supposed to keep track of everyone who tried out, what song they sang, and what scene they performed. Ms. Herbaut would make all the casting decisions, but she said she wanted to get my input as her official assistant director. There were about forty people ready to try out, a small core group of drama nerds who were busy doing scales and murmuring lines under their breath and everyone else who was trying out either for a lark or as a joke.

"Okay, we're ready to hear from . . ."—Ms. Herbaut looked down at the sign-in sheet—"Brenda Bauer."

For a second no one moved and I was afraid I would have to go over and drag Brenda up onto the stage, but then she stood and marched up, reverting to her lumbering, trademarked Frankenstein walk. She stopped in the center of the stage and blinked from the bright lights. I shot her a thumbs-up gesture and prayed she would get through the song without bolting from the stage. I was counting on her NASA dreams overpowering any nerves she had. If she wasn't afraid to be shot into space, then she ought to be able to handle this.

"Go ahead," Ms. Herbaut prodded as Brenda continued to just stand there. Brenda swallowed hard and then handed her music to the pianist at the side of the stage. When the music started she shut her eyes.

After much debate we had picked the song "I Don't Know How to Love Him" from the musical *Jesus Christ Superstar*. It had a sort of tragic-dreamy quality that worked well with Brenda's voice and had the added bonus of being a song I didn't think anyone else would pick. Brenda's voice wavered a bit when she started, but soon she hit her stride. I saw the pianist look up in surprise, and even the other students in the auditorium stopped goofing around and listened. When Brenda finished everyone fell silent. I could see her fidget on the stage.

"Who was that?" Ms. Herbaut said, shuffling the papers in her lap.

"Her name is Brenda Bauer." I paused, wanting to brag that I had been the one to convince her to try out, but I couldn't. As far as the rest of the school knew, we were nothing more than lab partners.

"Where has she been hiding for the past four years?" Ms. Herbaut whispered to me. "Brenda? That was lovely. Very lovely.

Would you mind doing another song for me, one from the show? I'd like to hear you do a duet with one of the other actors. Brian? Would you please join Brenda?"

Brian, one of the long-term drama nerds, gave a gallant nod and hopped up on the stage. It was then that I saw Christopher slouched down in a seat toward the back making notes. Ms. Herbaut had forbidden him to film any of the auditions as she thought it would make people too nervous. My stomach did a light flip when he looked up and met my eyes. I tucked a piece of hair behind my ear and tried to look official.

"I'd like to hear you two do 'On the Street Where You Live,'" Ms. Herbaut said to Brenda and Brian.

"I don't know the words to that one," Brenda said.

"I know them," Lauren said, standing up. "I've memorized the whole score. If you want to hear a duet, I can do it with Brian."

"Thanks, Lauren, but I want to hear Brenda right now. Brenda, why don't you and Brian go out into the hall and run through it, then come back when you're ready."

"No problem." Brian gave Brenda a reassuring smile and directed her through the wings, his hand on her elbow.

"I could do the song now," Lauren said again. I tried not to smirk when I heard Ms. Herbaut give a tired-sounding sigh.

"Okay, Lauren, how about you do your song while we wait for them to return?"

Lauren scampered up the steps and presented the music to

the pianist as if it were a royal decree. She took center stage, cleared her throat a few times, and then gave a solemn nod to the pianist to indicate she was ready.

Lauren sang well, but she should have waited. She should have gone after someone else who was merely mediocre so that she would stand out. Going right after Brenda only highlighted that her voice lacked something. Technically it was fine, she didn't miss a note, but it had no spark, no vitality. Partway through the song, you could see that she knew she was falling short so she sang louder and resorted to grand sweeping gestures with her arms when she felt it was needed. She bowed low when the song was over, and the group of devoted drama students gave her a quick smatter of applause even though they weren't supposed to.

"Thanks, Lauren," Ms. Herbaut said.

"I can do something else if you like," Lauren offered. "If you want to see my range, I can do one of the songs from the beginning. I've been working on a cockney accent too."

"We've got a lot of people to go," I reminded Ms. Herbaut. She surveyed the auditorium, calculating just how many renditions she was going to hear of "The Rain in Spain" before the afternoon was over.

"You're right. We're going to move along for right now, Lauren. I'll let you know if I need to hear another song."

Lauren pressed her lips together and her horse nostrils flared in annoyance. Not her best look. She caught me smiling and glared. I held my hands up and gave a silent clap. I'd let her take that any way she liked. I went back to riffling through my stack of papers to find who was supposed to go next. Ms. Herbaut called out for an Erin Legualt. One of the freshman girls jumped up and squealed as if she had been called as a contestant on *The Price Is Right*. As she ran for the stage she tripped over her own feet and fell. She popped right back up as if she were made from rubber. Ms. Herbaut massaged her temples. I'm guessing teaching drama at the high school level wasn't all Ms. Herbaut hoped it would be.

"Claire, can you take a bottle of water down to the pianist? It's going to be a long afternoon."

I gave her an "aye-aye, captain" salute and wove my way down the far aisle. I saw Brenda in the wings of the auditorium and I tried to give her a secret thumbs-up.

"HELEN!" Someone yelled out.

I spun around at the same time as another girl, both of us answering at the same time.

"What?"

The other Helen looked at me annoyed. Shit. I wasn't supposed to be Helen anymore. I could feel my face flushing red. Brenda looked at me strangely.

"I thought she said my name," I said to no one in particular. The girl next to me gave me an odd look, no doubt wondering how hard it was to tell the difference between the names Helen and Claire.

I practically tossed the water bottle at the pianist, fled for the safety of my seat, and smacked directly into Lauren. She was looking at me closely. I could see the wheels turning behind her eyes. Had she overheard the whole Helen thing?

"Excuse me," I said, as I moved past her. I could feel her eyes following me up the aisle. Shit. Shit. Shit. This is how things fall apart, stupid mistakes. Once I sat down I could see Lauren talking to one of the other drama kids, and the girl passed over a Tupperware container. Lauren marched back down the aisle and stood at the end of my row. I clutched my hands together so she couldn't tell they were shaking.

The Tupperware container was full of fruit diced into bite-size pieces, squares of cantaloupe and pineapple tossed with quartered frozen strawberries. Lauren thrust out the container in front of me.

"Have a piece of fruit," she said, her voice stern.

"No, thanks," I said.

"You should have some." Lauren pushed the Tupperware forward again so that it bounced against my chest. "Claire." I could feel my heart beating a thousand times faster. I was allergic to strawberries. Well, my Helen self was allergic and Lauren knew that. She had been with me when I had one of my worst allergic reactions as a kid. In fact, she caused it.

When we were nine or ten Lauren had the idea to do a science experiment where I tried strawberry-flavored gum to see if I would have a reaction, and then when I didn't, we tried a strawberry Fruit Roll-Up. The Roll-Up did me in, and I ended up throwing up with all the force of a fire hose. My mother had been livid. She couldn't believe I ate the Roll-Up just because Lauren asked me to when I knew I was allergic. She had no idea that at the time I would have done anything Lauren asked me. What's a little vomit between good friends?

I reached out and tentatively picked up a cantaloupe square.

"Have a strawberry," Lauren insisted with an impatient shake of the container.

Shit. She knows, or she thinks she knows.

"I actually love cantaloupe, it's my favorite," I tried.

"The cantaloupe isn't ripe. Have a strawberry. They're the best."

My fingers hovered over the berry and then before I could think about it too much I popped it into my mouth and swallowed it whole without chewing. Maybe chewing releases the allergic stuff; maybe if I swallowed it my stomach acid could kill it.

"Mmm, you're right. Those are great," I said.

Lauren's face fell. I could tell she thought she had me, but now she wasn't sure. I gave her a small salute with my clipboard and then made a vague motion indicating that she should head back to her seat. She walked back with her shoulders slumped. Once she sat down, she turned around every few moments and looked at me as if waiting to see what would happen. Christopher looked back and forth between us. I wondered what type of notes he was taking about us.

I pulled my purse up on my lap and started to rummage

through my stuff, hoping I might have some Benadryl in there. Nothing. I wondered if my throat would start to swell and if Brenda had covered enough in her science classes that she could do a trache on me using only a ballpoint pen if I needed one. I rubbed my fingers together, noticing that the tips that had touched the berry felt a bit hot and the skin tight. My stomach did a slow rollover. Uh-oh. I stood to make a run for the bathroom, and Lauren spun around again to look at me. I sat back down. If I went to the bathroom she would follow me—I knew it. She would know I'm allergic to the strawberry and she would know I'm not really Claire. The jig would be up, and I wasn't even close to reaching my goal of complete and utter Lauren destruction.

"Claire? Are you okay?" Ms. Herbaut touched my shoulder.

"Mmm-hmm." I smiled with my lips pressed together. I had the very real fear that if I opened my mouth to say anything that strawberry was going to come flying right out.

"I'll get us a couple of Diet Cokes. These auditions can be exhausting." She slid out of the row and down toward the cooler that was at the front. She motioned to the stage for things to continue.

Shit. Shit. Shit. The music started up for someone's tryout. The pianist was loud. My stomach rolled over again. I swallowed hard, trying to push the berry back into place. I broke into a cold, sticky sweat all over. My body was clearly planning to evict the berry and, from the way it felt, at a high rate of speed. I looked around for a solution. I gripped the handles of my purse. Then I glanced down. No way. I couldn't. I looked up again and saw the back of Lauren's head. I couldn't give up now.

Desperate times, desperate measures, I chanted to myself. I thought about how sometimes you need to sacrifice for what you really want. I dumped the contents of my handbag in my lap and then threw up in the purse. The piano drowned out the sound of my yakking. I sat back and wiped my mouth with a tissue. I even managed to smile at Lauren when she turned around for the millionth time.

I zipped the bag closed and placed it carefully back down onto the floor.

Maybe this would prove to the universe how serious I was about the whole thing.

Chapter Twenty-Seven

Grandma tapped on my door.

One of the downsides to having a grandma who used to be a social worker is that she's really into talking. She's not happy unless I'm blathering on about my feelings. She's always coming into my room so we can have these heart-to-heart talks. It's not that I don't appreciate it, but with my Lauren issues off the table for the discussion, I think she wanted me to have some new and interesting problem she could sink her teeth into. Sometimes I thought about making something up, like telling her I'd been considering a gender reassignment, just so we'd have something new to talk about. Grandma tapped on the door again and leaned her head into my room.

"There's someone at the front door for you."

I sat bolt upright in bed. "Someone for me?"

"Yes, it appears someone has discovered your lair despite your hermitlike existence."

I rolled my eyes and loped downstairs, hoping it wasn't Lauren. She would recognize my grandma for sure. Brenda was on the stoop holding a basket. She held it out.

"I made you cookies," she said.

I took the basket and looked inside. Chocolate chip, from the look of things.

"Why?"

"For helping me out, with the play and stuff. Plus I needed to talk to you. Ms. Herbaut called me at home. She's offering me the role of Eliza," Brenda said, fidgeting back and forth.

"Oh my God, that's great!" I did a small dance on our front step, mentally checking off another box on the revenge plan. This news was soooo worth the berry spew. I couldn't wait to see Lauren's face when she heard the news.

"I told her I wasn't sure if I wanted it," Brenda said, and my dance stopped mid-jig.

"You would be an amazing Eliza. What aren't you sure about?"

"It's just that drama means so much to some people, you know. Drama is their *thing*. I don't really care about it—it's just something to put on my transcript."

"So that you can be an astronaut, which *is* your thing," I pointed out. I took a bite out of a cookie and tried to think of a logical argument that would appeal to Brenda. "What made you worry about this anyway?"

"Christopher. He interviewed me for his film after tryouts

and he kept talking about how important it was to some people, how it was their dream, and I started to think maybe it doesn't matter if I do the play or not, or I could do a small part."

"Are you worried about Lauren? Trust me, she wouldn't worry about you." I wondered what Lauren had said to him during her interview. I bet she did that thing where she licked her lips when she talked. I hoped he was smart enough not to fall for that, but with guys you never know. They don't always do their thinking with their brains.

"Doesn't mean I shouldn't still do the right thing. Ms. H. says if I don't want the lead, she would want me to be the understudy for Eliza. I would still have something to put on my transcript, so it sort of meets my goals."

I didn't say anything. One more person who could play second fiddle to Lauren. I was so close. I had thrown up in my purse, for crying out loud, and now she wasn't sure she wanted this? My mind scrambled around trying to think of a reason why Brenda should take the role that didn't involve admitting that the whole thing was about Lauren.

"I think it's cool you're thinking of everyone else," I said. Brenda broke into a huge smile. "But . . ."—my voice trailed off and Brenda's face dropped—"I have to ask if you're sure you're turning down the part for the right reasons."

"What do you mean?"

"You've admitted that you hate being in front of groups. Are you sure you aren't backing down because you're scared?"

"Yeah, being in front of all those people freaks me out. But it's more than that. Why should I do it if the whole thing isn't that important to me?"

"Because challenging yourself is the important thing. I mean, don't take this the wrong way, but you're the kind of person who stays in your comfort zone. Look, you weren't sure if you wanted to cut your hair, right? You didn't care about it, so why bother? Right?"

"Yeah, I guess."

"And now that you cut it, are you glad you did?"

"Yeah."

"Well, this is like the haircut. Sometimes you aren't always sure why a challenge will make a difference, but you won't know until you take the leap."

"Take the leap, huh?"

"Full speed ahead, captain. If it turns out you hate doing the play, it's not like you have to do theater again, but how will you know if it's your thing unless you do it? Push yourself, gain the confidence." I realized I was starting to sound like one of those tacky motivational speakers so I shut up and hoped it worked.

"Do you really think I should?" Brenda asked.

"One hundred percent."

Brenda took a deep breath. "Okay, I'll do it."

"You will?"

Brenda laughed. "Don't sound so surprised. I trust you. If you think it's a good idea, I'll do it." The cookie I had eaten moments ago suddenly felt too big for my stomach. I tried to give her a reassuring smile. "I suspect Christopher will also be thrilled," she said. "I think 'science nerd-girl takes the lead' is good for his documentary."

"Not nerd girl, science-whiz woman," I countered.

"He asked me about you."

"What?"

"Well, that got your attention," said Brenda.

"Seriously, did he ask about me?"

"Yes, seriously, he did." Brenda picked a cookie out of the basket and began to nibble daintily on it. I tried to act like I didn't care what Christopher said. I managed to hold out for about three seconds.

"Are you going to tell me what he said?"

Brenda broke into a smile. "He thought it was cool you helped me with the audition. He wanted to know more about you, that kind of thing."

"What did you tell him?" I asked.

"I told him you were an international spy living under-cover."

"What?"

Brenda laughed. "No, I didn't say that. I told him that you were a hard person to figure out. Complex. You're like a black hole or the space-time continuum."

"I've never been compared to a celestial event before."

"You defy typical comparisons. He also mentioned that the

theater on the strip runs classic movies on Tuesday nights. He goes every week. In case I knew anyone who, you know, might be interested."

I felt my heart pick up speed. "He did, huh?"

"Yep." Brenda stepped down from the stoop. "I have to get going. I need to call Ms. H. back."

I sat on the stoop after she left. There was a part of me that wanted to drop the revenge thing—stop the lies and all the sneaking around so I could hang out with Brenda, have fun with the play, maybe watch some classic movies with Christopher.

I closed my eyes and remembered the moment I knew it was Lauren who had told the lie about me. I remembered how she looked in her backyard, her hair pulled back in a ponytail and the smug expression on her face. I remembered the instant that our friendship ended and that she hadn't cried a single tear over the whole thing. I thought about how she spun from one success to another and never took the time to think about the knife she'd stabbed in my back. It was time to put the heavy artillery into action. Lauren deserved to pay. What I wanted for my life wasn't important. Justice was on the line.

Chapter Twenty-Eight

The theater was in the middle of what Terrace called downtown. The year I moved away, the city council had decided that what the downtown needed was a makeover. Although it was no more substantial than a Hollywood set, the downtown now resembled a quaint New England town with fancy lampposts and lots of brick and wood storefronts.

I was surprised the movie theater was still around. It was small, built in the 1950s. Most of the big blockbuster movies were shown at the multiplex that was near the mall. My grandma told me the theater tried showing art films for a while, but Terrace isn't a town that is chock-full of people who go to see art films. Now it seemed to get by on showing second-run movies for cheap and, apparently, classic films on Tuesday nights. I had been looking forward to the movie all day. It was the cherry on top of an already almost perfect day.

Ms. H. posted the cast list outside the drama room first thing that morning. I had meant to get there early, but one of my grandma's friends had broken her hip the day before. Grandma had responded by pulling together a giant get-well basket that included tea, homemade muffins, a casserole, a few books, a couple of trashy magazines, and a card. She wanted me to drop it off at her friend's house before school. The package weighed approximately the same amount as a small hatchback car. I ended up missing all the action, but I certainly heard about it.

Once Lauren saw the cast sheet, she ran into the bathroom and refused to leave. She had the role of Henry Higgins's mother and—even better—was Brenda's understudy. Apparently people were all gathered outside the bathroom because they could hear Lauren crying and kicking the stall doors. When the school counselor heard about the fit she went into the bathroom, but Lauren wouldn't even talk to her. She stayed locked in a stall. Bailey and Kyla were called out of class to try and talk her down. They didn't have any luck with her either so someone called her mom. Mrs. Wood showed up in one of her fancy power suits in under ten minutes. She marched down the hall with a snarl on her face that she may have thought looked like a smile. The counselor cleared the bathroom and Lauren and her mom had a discussion. Kyla told me that you could hear Lauren's mom yelling from the hallway. Her mom was shouting at her to "pull it together" and "stop humiliating the whole family."

Fifteen minutes later, Lauren came out with her face washed clean, wearing a brittle smile. By the time I saw her at lunch she was insisting that she thought things had worked out for the best. Not having the lead would give her more time to focus on cheerleading—after all, she was the captain. You could almost believe her except for the fact that her face was completely frozen and her eyes looked a bit wide. She also kept giving a really high, loud laugh whenever anyone said anything, regardless of whether it was funny. She kept shooting glances over at Brenda, who was sitting surrounded by a bunch of the drama kids. Bailey and Kyla kept glancing at me behind Lauren's back when she wasn't paying attention. Kyla cocked one eyebrow, which I took as the universal sign for "whoa, look who's taken a one way trip on the *woo-woo* train."

I still hoped to see Lauren break down later in person, but she seemed to pull it more and more together as the day went on. I may not have liked her, but I had to give her credit. Lauren was a lot tougher than she looked.

I looked up at the marquee. For this week's classic film they were showing *The Thin Man*, starring William Powell and Myrna Loy. I had seen it on TV a few times. A great detective story set in the 1920s full of high society, martinis, and fabulous outfits. I paid for a ticket and went into the lobby.

The refreshment stand had all the usual snacks, but they were also selling vintage candy that you don't see anymore: Charleston Chews, Bottle Caps, Zagnuts, Necco Wafers, and Slo Pokes. Most of the people in the lineup seemed to be the senior set.

There wasn't anyone my age to be seen unless you counted the harried-looking girl with a metal hoop through her left nostril who was running the refreshment stand.

I slipped into the back of the theater and waited for my eyes to adjust to the dim lights. The movie was just starting and the light from the screen bounced off the faces of the people sitting there. The first face that I made out clearly was Christopher's. I slipped down the row and sat next to him. We both looked up at the screen and not at each other. He didn't say anything for a few minutes.

"Junior Mint?" He asked softly, shaking the box. I held my hand out, palm up, and he poured in a small pile of mints. He picked a mint out of my hand, and I could feel every nerve in my palm light up as his fingers touched me. When the mints were gone and my hand empty it seemed somehow right for him to fill it with his own hand. We held hands for the rest of the movie, and it was a good thing I had seen the movie before because I found it a bit difficult to concentrate. This was due in part to the proximity of Christopher and the fact that he was holding my hand, and in part to the elderly couple in front of who us kept whispering back and forth to each other. It appeared they shared one hearing aid. The elderly man spent the whole movie loudly whispering to his wife, "What did they just say?"

The only thing that would have made the night more perfect would have been if Lauren could have seen me with him. I loved old movies, but I almost wished we had gone to see something newly released. That way there would have been a greater chance of someone seeing us together and word getting back to Lauren. It was unlikely anyone here was going to spill the beans to her unless her grandma was in the audience.

When the lights came up, Christopher didn't rush to leave. He was a true film nut, the kind of person who wants to know every name on the lighting crew. When the final credit went by, we were the only people left in the theater.

"Have you seen the sequel?" he asked.

"*After the Thin Man?*"

"Creative titles weren't their specialty back in the 30s."

"As opposed to now, when we come up with the ever-unexpected *Spider-Man 2*," I pointed out.

"Touché." Christopher stood and began to lead us back out into the lobby. Everyone who worked at the theater nodded at him as we wove our way through. I had the sense he was a frequent visitor.

It was cold outside and Christopher let go of my hand to zip up his jacket. I stuck my hands in my pockets because it seemed sort of strange to let them just hang there in the freezing weather. Apparently, Terrace was skipping fall and moving directly into winter.

"I wasn't sure if you would come," Christopher said.

"You didn't exactly invite me," I countered.

"Then can I officially invite you for a cup of coffee?"

"No," I said, and then paused. "I'm more of tea drinker. Coffee makes me jumpy."

Christopher laughed. "We wouldn't want you jumpy."

We went in his car to the Bean There Café. The car was an ancient Honda that looked like it was held together with duct tape. What impressed me was that he never apologized for it the way so many people would. It was his car, and if you didn't like it then I suspect he would tell you to get out. When we walked in the café, another couple was just getting up from the two battered leather chairs that flanked the fireplace.

"Grab those seats and I'll get us some drinks," Christopher said. I reached into my pocket to pull out some money. I was going to have to get a new purse soon. I still hadn't replaced my bag since the whole projectile-strawberry incident. I had hoped if I washed it out well and used some Febreze it might somehow survive, but it was a lost cause. Not that I was complaining—the payoff had been worth it. I held out some money, but Christopher waved my cash away. "I think I can swing the tea."

I kicked my shoes off and folded up into the chair, my legs tucked under me. The fireplace was gas, more for show than anything else, but it did put out a bit of heat. The door swung open and a wave of cold air rushed into the room, but it was her voice that gave me the shivers. Lauren.

Bailey saw me first and waved like she was a plush Disney creature at the doorway to the Magic Kingdom and I was a guest from the Make-A-Wish Foundation. If they could bottle what Bailey had it would be better than Prozac. You usually didn't find people this happy unless there was serious medication support. Kyla held out her leg, and I couldn't figure out what she was doing until I realized she was wearing my boots. I shot her a thumbs-up. Lauren looked right past me.

"Hey, I tried to call you earlier," Bailey said, as they drew close. "We decided to go out and have a girls' night." She looked at me meaningfully and then over at Lauren. I'd missed out on a chance to cheer up Lauren, not that she needed cheering up—after all, she was just fine. She didn't want the part anyway, *blah blah blah.*

"My phone was off. I was at the movies."

Christopher turned around from the counter with our drinks. He walked over slowly and gave everyone a nod of recognition.

"Christopher!" Lauren said, her voice bright. "I guess you can't get enough of me—I see you everywhere these days. If this keeps up, I'm going to think you're following me."

"How could anyone ever get enough of you, Lauren?"

"Is that for me?" Lauren asked, gesturing to the extra cup he was holding in his hand. "How did you know I wanted hot tea?"

"It's for Claire."

Both Bailey and Kyla looked down at me. Kyla raised an eyebrow and I felt my face flush. Bailey looked so excited I thought she might levitate for a moment. I grabbed the tea and took a deep drink, the hot water searing my mouth. Lauren looked at Christopher and then at me. I suspect most people wouldn't know how upset she was, but I could see her nostrils flare out and the hitch in her chest as she tried to get a deep breath.

"Oops, sorry. Didn't mean to bust in on your big date," Lauren said, pausing to see if either of us would correct her.

"No worries." Christopher sank into the seat next to me.

"How are you feeling?" I tried to force my face into an expression that looked sympathetic.

"I'm fine." Lauren bit each word off.

"You sure? I know you must be disappointed. I think it's great you could go out with your . . ."—I paused to let the next word sink in—"girlfriends, and get your mind off of everything." Lauren's nostrils were nearly rippling with agitation. I touched the side of Christopher's hand to drive home the point that some of us weren't going to settle for being out with a girlfriend. Some of us had a date.

"Thanks for asking, but like I said, I'm fine." Lauren stomped over to the counter to order. Bailey and Kyla trailed after her. Bailey gave me an obvious okay sign with a wink that she must have imagined Christopher was incapable of seeing. Christopher waited until they had walked off.

"You know what I can't figure out?" he asked. "Why you and Lauren are friends."

I shrugged, not sure what to say. I couldn't bring myself to think of a single nice thing to say about her that would explain why anyone would be friends with her. I couldn't tell what he thought of Lauren. Did he think I was lucky to be in her sacred circle or an idiot to hang out with her? It was my duty to get him away from her clutches, before he fell under the Lauren spell that infected everyone else. He seemed flip with her, but I couldn't tell if it was meant to be friendly teasing or sarcasm tainted with disdain.

"I'm more friends with Bailey and Kyla."

"Sort of breaks up the holy trinity though, doesn't it? Those three have been thick as thieves since freshman year."

I shrugged again. At this rate he was going to think I was a conversational retard with shoulder spasms.

"What about you?" I said.

"What about me?"

"What do you think of Lauren?"

Christopher pulled back, surprise on his face.

"Lauren?"

"Yeah, do you like her?"

Christopher didn't say anything. He just looked at me. I felt someone else's eyes on me and turned to the side. Lauren, Bailey, and Kyla were sitting at a table. Bailey and Kyla were having a discussion, but Lauren was staring at me. If looks could kill I would have been six feet under with an ax in my head.

"I mean, I was just wondering," I added, turning back to Christopher. I touched his shoulder, making sure Lauren would get a good look.

"I don't think I'm her type," he said.

I took my hand off his shoulder. I noticed that he didn't say she wasn't his type.

"You don't seem to hang out with anybody," I said, dropping the whole Lauren topic altogether.

"Maybe I'm the kinda guy who likes my own company."

"Ah, a loner." I took a sip of my tea.

"Something like that," Christopher said, staring at me. I brushed the end of my nose to see if anything was there. He was staring so intently it felt like he had X-ray eyes, and I wasn't sure if I wanted him to see what was under the surface.

"What?" I asked finally.

"What do you mean?"

"I mean, why are you staring at me?"

"I thought girls were supposed to like it when guys looked into their eyes."

"Have you been reading *Cosmo*?" I teased.

"Nah, that magazine is trash. Besides, last time I read it, it promised '25 Ways to Drive Him Wild,' and I'm pretty sure only twenty-two of them would work."

I tried to laugh casually like I was used to joking around about sexual tricks with attractive guys, but the only thing that came out sounded like what would happen if someone stepped on a poodle.

"You okay?"

"Mmm, tea must have gone down wrong," I said. Christopher smiled and I had the sense that he knew I was lying. I couldn't tell if I wanted him to bring up the *Cosmo* article again or not. Part of me wondered, if I read the article, if I would be able to guess which three things out of the list didn't work for him.

"I can't quite figure you out," he said.

"Complicated, that's me."

"Something like that." He stared at me again for what seemed like forever. "You just don't fit into any single category."

"I tried to fit into someone else's definition once, but it didn't work out."

"Well, then you should stay unique." He leaned back in his chair so that we were sitting side-by-side facing the fire. His hand reached over and traced lazy figure eights on the side of my arm. Oh God, I hoped Lauren was catching a peek of this. Clearly if I was going to start a 25 Things to Drive Me Wild list, this would be in the top five. I wondered what would happen if I let out a moan right there in the coffee shop.

When my cell phone rang, I nearly jumped out of the seat. I yanked the phone out of my pocket so quickly that it flew out of my hand and landed in Christopher's lap. I grabbed it back without thinking. Christopher evidently wasn't expecting me to lunge at his crotch (I'm guessing that maneuver didn't make the *Cosmo* list), and he jumped up, splashing his coffee onto the floor. Everyone in the café turned to see what was going on. Lauren had already been looking over, only now I had given her something to smile about. I clicked the phone on. *It had better be an emergency.*

"Helen!" Grandma's voice bellowed into my ear. She sounded

surprised to hear me on the line, as if she meant to call someone else.

"Gram." There was a pause while neither of us said anything for a beat. I shot Christopher an apologetic smile. He was mopping up the coffee with a stack of napkins.

"I'm checking to see when you were planning to come home. It's a school night," Grandma said.

"I'll be home soon."

"Define 'soon.' It's already after ten."

"Gram."

"Helen."

I rolled my eyes at Christopher as if to explain the craziness that is my family. "I'll be home in an hour."

"Half hour."

"I'm a senior. In a year I'm going to be living on my own."

"Then in a year you can stay out as long as you like."

"I can take you back to your car now if you have to go," Christopher whispered.

"I'll be home in a half hour." I clicked off the phone before my grandma could begin her "the importance of boundaries" lecture.

"Sorry," I said, not sure if I was apologizing for the fact I had to go home or the fact that I'd grabbed him when the phone rang.

"No worries. I've got family too."

"I note yours doesn't call to check on you like you are a

five-year-old. It doesn't help that she used to be a social worker and worked with all these juvenile delinquents."

"What's her name? Maybe I know her."

I looked up, shocked.

"Joke. I'm joking."

I laughed to show that I knew that the whole time.

"Why does your grandma call you Helen?"

I choked on my tea when my throat seized shut. Christopher gave me a few whacks on the back.

"What?" I asked. Maybe if I stalled for time he would forget what he asked me, or maybe I could swallow my own tongue. I'd settle for a natural disaster, a small earthquake perhaps, anything to change the topic.

"I heard her on the phone. She called you Helen."

My brain scrambled around, looking for a good answer. "It's my great-grandmother's name." This answer had the benefit of being true, but the downside of being totally unrelated to what he'd asked me.

"Does your grandma confuse you with your great-grandmother a lot?

I laughed loudly like this was the best joke ever told. My mouth clicked shut when I saw his expression.

"It's my middle name too and she really likes it." I chewed on my lip. "You know, grandparents, they're weird . . . " My voice trailed off.

"Well, I better get you back to your car, Helen."

"Don't call me that," I said sharply. My eyes shot over to the corner to make sure Lauren hadn't heard him. "I mean, it drives me crazy when my grandma does it."

"Well, I wouldn't want to drive you crazy," he said, standing up. He walked toward the door and I followed him. Things had been going so well and I blew it by acting like a spaz. We drove back to my car in silence. When we got to the movie theater parking lot I waited a beat in case he wanted to do the arm-stroking thing again, but he kept his hands on the wheel.

"I had a nice time tonight," I said finally.

"Me too."

I waited to see if he would say anything else, like that we should do it again, but he just sat there.

"So, thanks for tea and telling me about the movie."

"They do the classics every Tuesday."

"Cool."

"Really? I thought you didn't like old movies." Christopher rubbed his chin. "What was it you said? You could take them or leave them?"

"I'm a girl. I'm supposed to change my mind." I flipped my hair. "Besides, didn't you tell me that you liked that I didn't fit into any one category?"

He didn't say anything. If I could stop acting like Claire and instead act like Helen, I somehow felt sure things would go better. I could admit I loved old movies too, and I wouldn't always have to be trying to cover things up. Of course, giving up Claire to go back to Helen would mean giving up getting revenge on Lauren. "I should go," I said finally.

"See you around."

I slipped out of his car and into my own. He waited for me to start my engine and then waved before driving off. I sat in the car thinking over the night. It was most likely for the best that he didn't try to kiss me. After all, I was out for revenge, not a relationship. The universe was going to get confused if I kept changing the goal. The important thing with Christopher was to keep him from Lauren, not to fall for him myself. The point of this year wasn't to have a relationship with anybody. Although I hadn't yet achieved the complete and total revenge that I had been hoping for, clearly things were starting to move in the right direction.

In theory I should be thrilled, so it wasn't clear why I felt like crying.

Chapter Twenty-Nine

Bailey and Kyla had potential careers as interrogators for the CIA. Bright lights and a cattle prod were the only things missing from their technique. The questions about my date with Christopher started in French class and continued straight through until lunch. By the time we sat down in the cafeteria every minute of the date had been broken down and we were now moving on to establish motivation.

"So when you held hands, did you take his or did he take yours?" Bailey leaned over the cafeteria table as if we were discussing espionage secrets. "I mean, who started things?"

"Who cares," Lauren asked, trying to change the subject. She had a smear of lipstick on her teeth. I noticed none of us had mentioned it to her. She wasn't eating at all, just drinking herbal tea.

"Are you kidding?" Bailey said. "Who took whose hand first is superimportant. It lets you know if he's taking control of the relationship or not. You can tell a lot from hand holding."

I popped a cherry tomato from my salad into my mouth. "It was somewhat of a meet in the middle. I had my hand out there, but he took it."

Bailey squealed. "I knew it! He likes you. He doesn't strike me as the kind of guy to hold hands with someone by accident."

I wondered if holding hands with someone by accident was something that came up a lot in Bailey's world.

"Pretty impressive, Dantes," Kyla said. "I can tell you, a lot of girls have had their eye on him. You move here and sweep him off his feet in record time. He must have been waiting for the right woman."

"Maybe. He didn't call last night and he hasn't said anything to me today," I pointed out.

Kyla waved away my concern. "Men. He has to prove he's independent. It's something to do with the testosterone they have. Let him come to you. Don't come across as easy. Play hard to get."

"Don't come across as easy? Interesting advice coming from you." Lauren smirked.

"What the hell is that supposed to mean?" Kyla asked, dropping her fork.

Lauren leaned back. She wasn't used to her lackeys speaking back to her. "Chill out. It was just a joke."

"Not funny. Maybe you're the one who shouldn't be giving out relationship advice," Kyla snapped.

All of us turned to look a few tables over, where Justin was sitting with Tiffany. She was an empty-headed sophomore girl who had more breasts than brains, but it was clear Justin had no trouble moving on post breakup.

"I said it was a joke." Lauren's face was flushed. "God, I was just sick of the conversation. They had one date and it wasn't even a real date—they bumped into each other at a movie. Excuse me if I don't want to spend my entire lunch hearing a blow-by-blow account."

"It's okay to be sad about your breakup." Bailey patted Lauren's arm. "But even if you're sad, you should still be happy for your friends."

Lauren wrenched her arm back. "Fine. I'm thrilled. The date sounds like it was freaking earth-shatteringly wonderful. I hope you have many more." She got up from the table and stormed out of the cafeteria.

"The prima-donna thing is getting old." Kyla stabbed a piece of lettuce. "She keeps that shit up and Justin isn't the only one who isn't going to want her around."

I waited a beat, but even Bailey didn't stick up for Lauren. Neither of them seemed remotely interested in following after her either.

I was still looking at the door where Lauren left when I saw Brenda standing with her tray a few rows over looking for a place. She smiled when she saw me. I spun back around. It wasn't that I didn't want to eat with her, but there was no way she could join this table. Not now. Not when things were going so well. My control on things was too fragile. The quickest way to stop being the center of this new orbit was to admit someone to the system who clearly didn't belong.

"So tell me again about what you guys talked about at the coffee shop," Bailey prompted.

Maybe it was because I had told the story at least six times already, but it felt like all the fun was washed out of it. I pushed my lunch away. I was getting sick of salad.

Chapter Thirty

*G*uilt is a funny thing. You end up undertaking all kinds of things you didn't picture yourself doing.

Brenda saw a posting about helping in the elementary school and got all excited. Something community service–related she could put on her applications. When she found out her assignment was helping second graders with an art unit, she convinced me to do the project with her. She didn't mention how I blew her off at lunch, but it was still there between us. Agreeing to do the project with her seemed easier than saying I was sorry. Certainly less complicated.

Brenda, being Brenda, did piles of research on art history and artistic techniques such as perspective and horizon lines. She hadn't counted on the fact that second graders are more interested in eating crayons than in learning how objects appear smaller when they are far away. There is a reason they make those things nontoxic. A group of second graders sat at our feet. A boy waved his arm madly. Brenda gave a sigh. He had already asked a few questions, and I could tell they weren't the kind of questions she had been hoping for.

"So the guy, van Gooey, who chopped off his ear, did he eat it?"

"His name was van Gogh. Wouldn't you rather hear about his paintings?"

"Did he chop off any other parts of himself?" He made some swipes in the air with his imaginary sword.

"Lots," I said, drawing out the word. "By the end of his career all that was left was one eye and a thumb."

"Cool," he whispered. Brenda shot me a look. The teacher wasn't paying any attention at all. She was sitting in the back of the room reading *People*. We could have taught a class on sex education and she wouldn't even have noticed. We could have had a room full of second graders strapping condoms on some bananas and she wouldn't even have looked up from an article on George Clooney.

"Claire is joking around with you. He didn't chop off anything else. Maybe somebody else has a question about art?" Brenda looked around the room with a hint of desperation in her eyes.

"If you eat green crayons, will you poop green?" the same boy asked. The class burst into giggles.

Brenda gave up and slumped down on the stool the teacher had provided.

"No. Trust me on this, because I've tried. It also doesn't work if you eat poster paints," I said.

"Gross," a little girl who had at least a dozen barrettes in her hair said.

"Very gross," I agreed.

"Way back then it was a time of artistic turmoil with competing views of what made something art," Brenda said, still trying to educate tomorrow's leaders on more than ear chopping and colored poop. The kids all turned to look at her and then back at me for clarity.

"'Turmoil' means really screwed up. No one could agree. It's like how some people think SpongeBob is funny and other people think he's disgusting."

"You know what, let's skip the rest of the art history lesson and go right into doing our own art!" Brenda said, changing gears. She pointed toward their desks, which had been pushed together in little islands around the room. The teacher had covered the desks with large pieces of paper and there were jars of bright poster paints sprinkled around. "We're going to break into groups and paint pictures. We talked about all kinds of art today—landscapes, still life, portrait, and abstract. You can choose to paint whatever you want. This is what we call artistic freedom."

"Can I paint people chopping off each other's ears?" Guess Who yelled out. I was starting to think that kid was going to grow up to be a serial killer. If I lived in his neighborhood, I would keep a close eye out for pets going missing in the area.

Brenda looked at the teacher for some guidance. She had to clear her throat several times before the teacher looked up.

"No, Richard, you may not paint chopped-up people," the teacher said in a bored voice before she went back to paging through her magazine.

"But then I'm not free," Richard said, indicating that he grasped the concept of artistic freedom, which I would have guessed was way above the second-grade brain.

"That's right. You're not free. You're in second grade," the teacher said.

Richard kicked the carpet in frustration but went to sit at his desk. We stayed to help for a while. I would have stayed all afternoon. I like kids. It's way easier to navigate elementary school than high school. Here I could be totally me. I didn't have to worry about keeping up the Claire front. Being popular took so much energy. You had to smile at the right people, or risk being labeled a stuck-up bitch, and ignore the wrong people, or be labeled a loser lover. Besides, I like the way poster paints smell. When our time was up, the teacher gave us each a candy bar to thank us for coming down. Brenda tried to tell her that we didn't mind at all, but I just said thank you. "Never turn down free chocolate" is one of my mottos.

I unpeeled the Kit Kat as we walked down the hall. I broke off one of the bars and handed it over to Brenda.

"Thanks for inviting me. It was fun, and not just because I got out of math," I said.

"And you can put it on your college applications."

"Right."

"You know there's still time to apply places."

I nodded absently. I had a bunch of applications piled on my desk at home, but it seemed surreal that I was expected to just figure out where I wanted go, pick a major, and come up with some sort of plan for my life. How was I supposed to know what I wanted to do? How could the adults in my life, who didn't trust me to choose to do the right thing after midnight, think I was supposed to make this kind of decision?

"I may take a gap year."

"What would you *do?*" Brenda's nose wrinkled up in confusion.

"I don't know. That's sort of the point of a gap year, isn't it? To sort out what you want to do, have a gap."

"You should apply to Boston University. Then if I get into MIT we'll be in the same city."

"Yeah, maybe." I couldn't imagine anything after this year. Everything had been about Lauren for so long that it was like I couldn't imagine what would follow. Where my future should be, there was just a blank screen.

"We could get an apartment or something together after a year or two. My folks really want me to live in the dorms for a while though."

"I don't think you should count on me to be there for you," I said.

Brenda looked over at me. "I'm getting that sense."

"Look, it isn't that I don't want to hang out with you more. It's just that I can't. There's all this stuff going on. Stuff I have to sort out."

"So who hurt you?"

"No one hurt me."

Brenda gave a disbelieving snort. "You don't have to tell me if you don't want to, but I can still tell. You don't let anyone get close to you. The thing is, no one can hurt you unless you let them."

"If you think that, then no one has ever really burned you," I pointed out.

"I don't mean to make it sound simple. It's just that if you hold on to a hurt then you never get over it. It's like picking at a scab."

"Let's stop talking about my scabs, okay?"

"But if you want to move on then you have to let go of what is holding you back."

"Look, Oprah, I asked you to drop it," I snapped.

"Friends look out for each other," Brenda countered.

"I didn't ask you to look out for me. In fact, I specifically told you there was stuff I didn't want to talk about, but all you do is push. Stop trying to make me into your friend." Brenda stopped walking and looked at me, her eyes wide. "What? I thought things only hurt if you let them," I said.

Brenda's head snapped back like I had slapped her. I wished I could rewind time and take back that last sentence. If I was Helen I would, but I still had to be Claire. At least a bit longer.

Lauren was so close to cracking. Brenda didn't say anything else, just marched back toward the high school. Her shoulders drew up under ears and she started to do that weird Frankenstein lurch that she had just about given up. I watched her walk away, then kicked the wall.

Chapter Thirty-One

Christopher was leaning against my car after school. He had this way of standing like his limbs were just barely connected, sort of loose.

"Do you like parties?" Christopher asked as I walked up.

The real answer to the question was that I didn't know. It was one of those things where I hadn't been invited to many in the past couple of years. However, Claire would have been to a zillion. I put a hand on my hip. "It depends on who's at the party."

"Do you want to come to one with me tonight?" Christopher asked.

"Like a date?" I hated how my voice came out all high and screechy.

"That's what I'd been thinking. I thought maybe we'd give the whole being together outside the movie theater thing a try."

"I do better in the dark." As soon as the words came out of my mouth I knew it didn't come across like I meant.

"Well, that sounds promising."

"I meant, I had a good time at the movie. You know, dark theater." I decided I better change topics. "Who else is going to the party?"

"So are you saying you don't want to go with me to the party unless your friends are there?"

"No, that's not what I meant." I didn't add that while I wanted to go to the party with him, I especially wanted to go if Lauren could see us together. "I'll go."

"Well then, it's a date," Christopher said with a smile. He took a step forward and then paused. He was going to kiss me. My heart started to beat super fast like I was running a sprint. His hand reached over and cupped the end of my elbow, pulling me just a touch closer. I swallowed. *God, I hope I don't have Kit Kat caught in my teeth.* That's all I needed, for him to kiss me and end up finding a snack in there. No one likes secondhand chocolate. If I'd known he was going to kiss me, I would have gone to the bathroom and swished out my mouth first. I closed my eyes and I could feel his breath as he leaned in. His breath smelled like mints.

HONK!

We both jumped back. A car driving by gave another loud honk and someone leaned out the window, yelling at a kid on the school steps.

"Joe! Suck this!" The kid in the passenger seat turned around and pressed his butt cheeks against the window. The pasty butt, quite hairy I might add, had a way of taking all the romance out of the moment. Christopher apparently felt the same way as he was rubbing his palms on the front of his jeans nervously and showing no signs of coming back in for a kiss.

"Yeah, so . . ." I wasn't really sure what to say, so the sentence sort of trailed off.

"Yeah." Christopher looked at me and then away. "How about I pick you up at your house around six? Julie Baker's parents are out of town and she's doing a sort of barbecue thing."

"Sounds good."

Christopher gave me a nod and walked off. It was framing up to be a very interesting evening.

Popularity Question: How do you know if a high school party is successful?

1. There is at least one person throwing up outside in the flower beds.
2. So many people have come that someone thought it would be a good idea to start parking on the lawn.
3. A minimum of three couples are having sex somewhere in the house—at least one of them in the parents' bed.
4. Doritos, chips, and other salty snacks have been crumbled into a fine powder and ground into the living room rug.

5. At least one priceless breakable has been broken. Someone will make an attempt to fix it with superglue or toothpaste. It will not work.
6. The kitchen floor will be sticky from spilled liquids, making it possible for a small freshman to become completely stuck to the floor like to a giant piece of flypaper.
7. Music is playing at a level loud enough to cause ears to bleed. Occasionally someone will yell to turn it down before the neighbors call the cops. This person will then be called a pussy by the others and the music will go a notch louder.
8. A group of jocks will be around the dining room table, playing a complicated drinking game to which no one completely understands the rules. It is possible that the rules are completely irrelevant anyway.

In the case of Julie's party, it was all of the above. Julie didn't seem to mind. She was wandering through the house wearing her mom's silk kimono-style bathrobe and drinking a wine cooler. It was possible that she had decided she was going to get the death penalty for the party when her parents got home so she might as well enjoy her final night on earth.

Lauren was already at the party. When Christopher and I arrived it was clear she'd had quite a few drinks. It looked to me like she'd left drunk behind a few beers ago and had moved into that stage where your brain starts to float free in all the alcohol.

Lauren lunged at Kyla declaring her to be her "very best friend in the world!" Kyla met my eyes across the room and shook her head in disgust. It didn't look like Bailey was there. I wondered who Lauren was counting on to hold her hair out of the toilet when she started puking, because it was clear to me that Kyla was not going to volunteer.

Christopher and I wove our way through the crowd of people until we found the cooler in the kitchen. He grabbed a beer for himself and then looked over at me.

"Is there any Diet Coke left?" I asked.

Christopher fished through the melting ice water and pulled out a can, taking the time to pop the top for me. And people say there are no gentlemen left.

We clinked our drinks together and wandered out onto the back porch where at least it was quiet enough to hear yourself think. The porch was screened in so it wasn't quite as cold as being outside, but it was still way colder than the house. You could see your breath in the air.

"You cold?"

I started to shake my head no and then realized there was no point in being polite; my shivering was most likely giving things away. Christopher pulled off his military jacket and wrapped it around me. It was a deep olive green wool and still warm from his body.

"Better?" he asked.

"Much."

We sat on the bench, watching people come and go through the kitchen. I knew I should talk about something, but I was at a complete loss to come up with a topic. The longer I didn't talk, the louder the silence was between the two of us. What if we had nothing to talk about but movies? Did that mean our relationship was doomed? Would it be easier to talk to him if I was being myself, or was he only interested in me because I was Claire? Maybe it didn't matter who I was because I was doomed in any relationship due to my lack of communication skills. There was a constant loop in my head, *say something, say something, say something, say something.*

"So did you know Katharine Hepburn did all her own stunts? She thought the stunt women didn't stand up straight enough," I blurted out. I then wished for a meteor to suddenly fall from the sky and take me out for saying something so completely random. That's the problem with space debris. It never causes a cataclysmic event when you want it to.

"I can honestly say that no, I didn't know that," Christopher said, no doubt taking pity on my poor social skills. "I would have thought it was part of the job requirement for stunt people to have good posture."

"Yeah. It could have just been her take on stuff. She was sort of a control freak about things. I mean, the guy I used to date who was into movies told me she was," I tried to explain while still waiting for the earth to swallow me whole.

"I always had the impression she wasn't the kind of person to be wishy-washy on issues." Christopher took a drink of his beer.

"What's wrong with knowing exactly where you stand on things?"

"Life isn't a vintage film," Christopher said. When he saw my confused face he explained, "Things aren't black-and-white."

"Some things are."

Christopher gave a vague one shoulder shrug. "Don't get me wrong. I like Katharine Hepburn. She was honest. You knew where she stood."

I swallowed. I wondered what he would think of my less-than-honest take on key issues like my real identity.

"I have no idea why I brought up Katharine Hepburn," I admitted.

"Don't worry. Random isn't a bad thing."

"The thing is, I'm not really good at this kind of thing."

"Just so we're on the same page, what kind of thing are we talking about?" Christopher asked, taking a long drink of his beer.

"Being with people."

"I thought it came second nature to the elite crowd," Christopher said.

"Sometimes it only looks like it comes easy. It can be a lot of work."

For some reason I had the urge to tell him about Lauren. About what she did and how it made me afraid to get too close to anybody. I don't know why, but I was sure he would know what to say, that he would have some kind of advice. I wanted to explain that I had been sure things were black-and-white, but lately there was all this gray everywhere. I opened my mouth to tell him when the door to the patio flew open and Julie spilled out. She spotted us and swayed back and forth while her mouth waited to catch up to whatever her brain was thinking.

"You guys have to come inside, we're playing a game," Julie said, though it came out more like, *"You'll gooz, come inziiid, waa plainning a guum."*

It was possible that an out of control party was not the place to spill your guts. Unless you counted Lauren, who dashed past all of us to spill her guts in the bushes in a nonmetaphorical sense.

Christopher stood up and took a step toward Lauren and then stopped. There wasn't anything he or anyone else could do to help.

"Splashdown!" one of the jocks yelled out the living room windows. I glanced over my shoulder. It looked like everyone was getting a good view of Lauren.

"Those are my mom's azaleas," Julie slurred.

"Not her finest hour," I said.

"What's your problem with Lauren?" Christopher asked.

"I don't have a problem."

"You spend a lot of time worrying about something that isn't a problem."

"I have no idea what you're talking about." I didn't meet his eyes. "Do you want to go inside and play a game?" I tried to make my voice sound flirty.

"You know, unlike most people, I'm not real big on playing games." He turned around and walked away.

Chapter Thirty-Two

*C*hristopher and I didn't stay at the party late. Things had started to go downhill rapidly once Lauren started throwing up. It's been my limited party experience that once people start spewing bile in public the fun is over.

Christopher pulled into my grandma's driveway but didn't turn off the car. It looked like our second date was over.

"I had a good time," I said.

"Really?" Christopher stared out the window.

"You don't believe me?"

"Honestly? No." He looked over at me. His face was tinted blue in the dashboard lights. "I don't know what to believe. Sometimes I get you and other times it seems complicated."

"Complicated can be interesting."

"It can also be a lot of work."

I wasn't sure what to say. Claire would have a flip comment about how some things are worth a bit of work, but I wasn't sure the line would work on Christopher. My grandma flicked on the driveway light indicating that she thought enough time had passed out there.

"I guess I should go."

"Have a good night."

I paused, wanting to say something else, but the lights flicked on and off again. "You have a good night too."

I replayed the night as I lay in bed. Public vomiting was a new low for Lauren. It was one thing for a popular girl to get a little wild and wacky at a party. It was a whole other dimension when you started spewing for the world to see. There was no official way to tell, of course—popularity doesn't have an official ranking list that can be checked—but I was almost certain Lauren's reign was at an end. She wasn't unpopular. It would take a lot more hurling for that to happen, but she was definitely less popular. I was one step closer to total victory, but it didn't feel nearly as good as I had hoped. Instead of the image of Lauren hurling in the bushes for all to see, the picture in my mind was Christopher looking disappointed.

I rolled over and looked at the digital clock—3 a.m. I clicked on the bedside lamp and pulled my revenge binder out from under the bed. I ran my finger down the list. Lauren had lost her boyfriend, the lead in the play, and her friends. Christopher hadn't been hers, and he wasn't exactly mine now either, but no way could he find her attractive after what she pulled tonight. The only thing left was cheerleading, and I even had finally come up with a plan for that. I should feel like celebrating. Something was missing. I ran through the list over and over trying to determine if I had left anything out, some angle on the plan that would click everything into place.

Then I saw it. I looked down at the binder. It was all about Lauren, what she had, what was important to her. Pages and pages all devoted to the great Lauren Wood. Maybe I needed a list about me for a change.

I pulled out a clean sheet of paper and wrote across the top: LIFE AFTER LAUREN.

I stared at the paper. There she was, right at the top of my list. I crossed off her name with a thick line. Nope. I scribbled over it. That wasn't right either. No way was I letting her ruin my list. I crumpled up the paper and tossed it toward my trash can. I grabbed a fresh sheet of paper and started again. LIFE LIST.

Now all I had to do was make a list of things I wanted to accomplish. Things I wanted for myself. I tapped my pen on the edge of the binder, waiting for inspiration. After a few minutes I wrote down a couple of items:

1. Friend.

It went without adding that I meant a real friend. Someone I could count on, someone like Brenda.

2. Christopher.

I was willing to admit it. I liked him. I wanted him to like me. The real me.

I stared at the list. Two items? That's it? How could I have only two things that I wanted out of my life? It has been easier coming up with things to take away from Lauren than it was to come up with what I wanted for myself. The only other item I could think of for the list was too vague. I wanted to be happy.

I added another item to my list:

3. Get a Life.

Chapter Thirty-Three

I tried to call Brenda on Sunday night, but her cell wasn't on. I called her home number but her mom said she was studying and couldn't be disturbed. The thing with Brenda is she's the type who really could be into studying, all caught up with protoplasm or black holes, and not want to be disturbed, but I had a hunch that wasn't the issue.

I'd made a decision. I didn't want to hear a blow-by-blow replay of the party from Lauren's perspective. I didn't care what Kyla thought of what everyone was wearing. I had zero interest in spending another lunch pretending to find what they said even remotely interesting. Getting revenge on Lauren didn't have to mean giving up everything that I wanted for myself. At lunch on Monday, I gave the three of them a nod and then walked right past their table.

I stood at the front of the tables and searched up and down looking for Brenda. I wanted to talk to her about Christopher, and I also owed her an apology for always blowing her off in public. I looked right past her at least three or four times, not recognizing her. She was sitting at a table with a bunch of other girls from the play. She was wearing one of her new outfits and laughing at what one of the other girls said.

"Hey, there you are," I said as I walked up to her. Brenda looked up as if she didn't know who I was.

"Oh, hi."

I stood there with my tray wondering if she was going to ask me to sit down.

"I tried to give you a call last night."

"I was studying." Brenda's eyes didn't meet mine.

"Oh." The whole table sat there watching me. "Mind if I join you?" I asked.

"We're just finishing up actually," Brenda said.

I looked down at their trays. Unless they were on the anorexic diet, Brenda was dissing me. They hadn't even made a dent in their lunches. My jaw tightened. So that was how it was going to be.

"Fine. Now that I think about it, I've lost my appetite anyway." I walked to the end of the row and dumped everything, including the tray into the garbage and walked out. I slammed open the bathroom door, and once I was sure I was alone, I kicked the stall door. It swung open, whacking into the toilet paper dispenser, and then bounced shut again. It was not nearly as satisfying as I had hoped and it made my foot hurt. I gave it another kick anyway.

I heard the door open and before I even turned around I knew it was Brenda.

"I thought you weren't done with lunch," I said, hating how my voice sounded snotty.

"You can't do this, you know."

"Do what?"

"Act like you're my friend one minute and then not the next moment. Tell me you know exactly what I need to do and then the second I have any advice for you, tell me that I have no business giving it." Brenda tossed her hands in the air.

"I know," I said.

"I'm not interested in being friends with you if you're going to be all CIA. *I'd tell you, but then I'd have to kill you.* I don't even know if you *want* to be my friend."

My throat felt like it was getting more and more narrow. It felt like she was asking me to step out onto the window ledge of a tall building.

Brenda rested her hand on my arm. "I don't want to do all this back and forth. Friends one minute and then not the next. If you want me to understand that there are things you can't do, you should be willing to understand there are things I can't do."

"So where does that leave us?" I asked.

"What do you know about space walks?" Brenda said.

"Space walks? Is this your subtle way of changing the subject?"

"Stick with me and it'll make sense. What do you know about space walks?"

"My knowledge here is pretty slim."

"Here's the thing, space isn't built for humans. It's freezing cold;

there's no air. So the astronaut gets all dressed up," Brenda said.

"I'm not a complete idiot. I know people don't just go walking around in outer space."

Brenda ignored me. "So the astronaut goes into an air lock. It's sort of a waiting room. They suck the oxygen out, and then when the pressure is equaled they can go outside the spaceship, and then they do the same thing in reverse when they want to come back in. It isn't instantaneous. The transition takes some time. Go too fast and someone could get hurt; go too slow and you could run out of time."

"What does this have to do with us?" I asked.

"You asked where we are—we're in the air lock."

"Waiting for the pressure to equalize," I said.

"Exactly, and hopefully before we run out of air." Brenda turned around, and suddenly my chest felt tight like it was going to burst, and I had to do something to release the pressure. Before I knew it the words flew out of my mouth.

"My name isn't Claire."

Brenda turned around and looked at me with one eyebrow up.

"My name is Helen." My voice shook as I said my real name.

The first bell rang. Lunch was over.

"I'm guessing this isn't the kind of story that can be wrapped up in the next three minutes, huh?" Brenda said with a sigh.

Chapter Thirty-Four

One of the benefits of being generally good is that the teachers trust you. Brenda marched down to biology and told Mr. Wong that we needed some time to work on our bacteria project. He gave her the keys to the lab and wrote us a pass in case anyone wondered why we weren't in class.

The biology lab was dark. The blinds were drawn so everything had that sort of hazy shadow lighting. Brenda and I sat on opposite sides of one of the lab tables facing each other. I held on to one of the microscope cords, winding it up one finger and then letting it go so it hung like a giant spiral curl, and then I would do it again. If you were going to film a horror movie, the empty lab would be a great place for it: posters of eviscerated frogs on the wall, strange chemical smells, trays of dissection tools off to the side, and microscopes casting giant shadows on the far wall like a line of marching Tyrannosaurus rexes. Then again maybe the room wasn't scary and it was just the fact that I was scared out of my mind.

"So . . ." Brenda's voice trailed off.

"I don't know where to start."

"Why don't you start with why you're calling yourself Claire if your name is Helen."

"Would you believe me if I told you I busted up a mafia drug ring and that I'm in the witness protection agency?"

"No," Brenda said, sitting perfectly still.

"Okay, I'll tell you, but you have to promise that you will never tell another soul."

"You want me to swear on a Bible or something?"

I grabbed a copy of our biology textbook off the table and passed it over to her. "I want you to swear on science, on Mr. Darwin here. It's that important to me."

Brenda placed one hand on the science textbook and raised her other hand. "I swear on this science textbook that I will keep whatever secret you tell me."

I took a deep breath and tried to sort out the story in my mind. "It started from the moment I was born."

It took me nearly forty minutes to tell her everything, how Lauren and I had been friends, what she did to me, and my master plan to get revenge.

"*You're* the Snitch Bitch?" Brenda asked sounding almost impressed. "I remember hearing about that freshman year.

Everyone was talking about how you had screwed over the seniors."

"I'm not the Snitch Bitch, Lauren is. So do you see now why I had to do this?"

"So you broke up her relationship with Justin?"

"Sort of. I mean, I put the pieces into place."

"And you poisoned her mascara?"

"Poison is a bit harsh. That stuff is just an irritant," I pointed out.

"But you also ripped her jeans." I nodded. "Took her shoes." I nodded again. It was only one shoe, but whatever. "You're sabotaging her friendships and trying to make sure her crush ignores her." Brenda looked vaguely in shock. I wasn't sure what she thought my secret was going to be, but I was pretty certain this wasn't it. "So everything you're doing this year is designed to get revenge on her."

"Yeah."

"What about me? Where do I fit in?" Brenda asked.

"What do you mean?"

"I mean how do I fit into your revenge plan?"

"You're not part of the plan. We met and I liked you," I said.

"So you didn't give me a makeover and get me to try out for the play with the goal of keeping Lauren from getting the part?"

"Uh," my voice stuck in my throat. "That wasn't just about revenge. I mean, I did think you would be really good, and you are. Really good."

"How lucky for you that you could help me out and screw over Lauren at the same time. Very efficient."

"Don't be mad. I should have told you, but I swear I thought it was a killer idea for you to do the play. I still do."

"Because it helps you out?" she asked.

"No. Honest now, are you liking it?" Brenda gave a deep sigh and I pressed on. "See, you do like it, don't you? It's fun," I said. "Not to mention it's going to look great on your applications."

"Yes, it's fun, and yes, I'm glad I did it, but you should have told me there was more to it."

I stood up and paced up and down the aisle. "You wanted to know, you made me tell you, and now you're mad."

"I think I'm entitled to be a little annoyed to find out you've used me."

"I am not using you," I said, my voice rising.

"I want you to leave me out of this plan from now on."

"Deal."

"I am sorry about what happened, the whole Snitch Bitch thing. What she did was lousy. You didn't deserve that," Brenda said.

I felt my eyes fill up. One nice word from her and I was ready to burst into tears. I shrugged instead of saying anything because I was pretty sure I would start crying if I opened my mouth.

"So when will you be done with this plan?" Brenda asked.

"When I've got revenge."

"How much is enough?"

"I don't know. It seems like I'm close. She's starting to fall apart. If I can push her just a little bit further then I think she'll crash and burn." I crumpled up a bunch of extra handouts that were on the table and chucked them into the trashcan.

"You want her to suffer."

"Exactly!" I pounded my palm down on the lab table. At last someone understood.

"What if she doesn't? What if you do your best to make her life miserable and it doesn't work?"

"Thanks for the vote of confidence."

"I'm being serious. How do you even know if you've won? What does revenge mean? It's just a vague concept. It doesn't mean anything," Brenda said.

"It means a lot to me."

"Okay, say you win, whatever that means. What in your life is going to be different after you get your revenge?"

I looked at her and opened my mouth, but I didn't know what to say so I went back to pacing back and forth for a minute while Brenda watched me. I looked over at the periodic table poster on the wall just in case there was an answer in there for me.

"What I'm trying to point out is that I totally understand why you would want revenge on Lauren, but it doesn't gain you anything," Brenda said.

"Satisfaction. A sense of justice," I offered, but in the back of my mind when she had asked what I wanted to gain, an image of Christopher floated in my mind.

"And then? I mean, unless you're willing to kill her, then whatever you do, she'll just get over it eventually. She'll move on." Brenda paused, giving me a careful look. "You aren't planning to kill her, are you?"

"No, I'm not going to kill her. Maim her maybe, a nice amputation or something." Brenda's eyes grew wide and I had to fight the urge to roll my eyes. "I'm not going to maim her either. I want to do something that will hurt her like she hurt me." I didn't mention that I already had put something into place that might just do the trick. Something that would get Lauren kicked off the cheerleading team and humiliate her all at the same time. I had the sense Brenda wouldn't want to know the details. Besides, I'd already planted the evidence in Lauren's purse.

Brenda sat at the lab table without moving. She had her hands folded on the table, and she was looking at them like they were a crystal ball with all the answers.

"I'm glad you told me."

"I'm glad too." I was about to say something else, but Brenda waved me off. She had more to say.

"I understand why you want to do this, but I have to tell you, I think it's a bad idea. If you want real revenge then live a great life, prove that what she did didn't matter that much. The fact that it still bothers you just makes her win last longer," Brenda said.

"You sound just like my grandmother. I can't explain it. This is just something I have to do," I said. Brenda was chewing on her lower lip. "I'm not going to be able to move on until I finish this. You're going to keep this secret, right?"

"I really don't think this is a good idea."

"You've made that pretty clear, but you promised. You promised on Darwin." I held up the book as a reminder.

"What if she gets hurt?"

"As much as it would give me great joy, I am not going to slip arsenic into her salad."

"What about what you did with her mascara? What if she had permanent eye damage?"

"Makeup companies have to make their products idiot-proof just in case someone sticks lip gloss in their eye by accident. Having chili pepper extract in your eye might hurt, but it isn't going to damage anything. That's why they test all that stuff. Better living through science and all that."

"I don't know."

"I'm not asking for you to help me with it, just to not say anything. I'm almost done. There is just one more thing I have to check off. We don't ever have to talk about it again. I'll move on. You can help me apply for colleges and all that stuff."

Brenda gave this big sigh. "I won't say anything." She looked over, meeting my eyes. "I promise."

I felt a huge weight lift off my shoulders. She was right, it did feel good to have told someone. It made me feel less alone even if she did think the whole plan was insane.

"You have to promise me something too," Brenda said. "Think about the law of diminishing returns."

"Huh?"

"Is all the effort you're putting into your plan worth it? In science sometimes researchers have to realize they've gone down the wrong path and turn around before they get further from what they really want. And one more thing," Brenda said.

"What?"

"I don't feel good about lying to Mr. Wong. We need to put in at least an extra hour on our biology project after school to make up for this hour."

"I will gladly spend an hour with you and your bacteria."

"Our bacteria."

I broke into a smile. "Of course, our bacteria." I reached over and we shook on the deal.

Chapter Thirty-Five

I took everything off the kitchen shelves. The one downside of my grandmother's cooking habit is that she never throws anything away. She wants to be sure she has everything she might need to make any meal should all grocery stores across the county suddenly go out of business. She had drawers full of spices (cilantro, basil, fennel seed, coriander), different types of flour (cake, unbleached, whole wheat, enriched, multigrain), sugar (brown, white, castor, powdered, colored), and countless varieties of vinegar and oil. When I had gotten home from school I'd wandered around the house, practically bouncing up and down with nervous energy. The conversation with Brenda kept playing over and over in my mind. That's when tackling the kitchen occurred to me.

Once I had everything off a shelf, I wiped it down first with warm water to get all the sticky and spilled bits up and then with a quick spray of the kitchen cleanser. I had been at it so long a cloud of bleach hung over the room. While I cleaned I wondered what

Christopher was up to. I couldn't quite figure out what we were doing. Sometimes it seemed like he liked me. He'd held my hand at the theater and I would have sworn we were close to kissing at least twice. Then there were other times when I wasn't sure if he liked me at all. He was like this ghost; he drifted in and out of my life. Sure, I could call him, but it seemed like it should be his move next.

It was possible that he was busy with his film and that's why he didn't call. Instead of being annoyed, I should have admired him for having so much creative drive. I knew he had interviewed the whole cast because Brenda told me. He hadn't asked me for an interview, but it's possible that director flunky wasn't an important enough role to merit film time.

"What'd you do?" My grandma asked, surprising me. I was standing on the kitchen counter and turned so quickly I almost fell over.

"I thought you were going to the hospital to visit Kay," I said.

"I've been around a long time, kiddo. Don't think I didn't notice that you didn't answer the question."

"My parents like it when I help out without being asked."

"Uh-huh. You're their only kid, so they don't know any better. I had three, plus six grandkids. You don't get to be my age without knowing teenagers don't voluntarily clean out the kitchen cupboards."

"Well I do."

My grandma fixed me with a look and then shook her head.

She sat at the counter and started sorting through the mail. My parents had sent a postcard. She flipped it over to read the short note and then stuck it on the fridge.

"You see this from your folks? Sounds like things are going well."

I gave a nod and focused on the shelf. Some Karo syrup had spilled and created some type of chemical bond with the wood.

"Sometimes I clean because it feels like the only way I can make order out of something," she said. "When my life gets confusing, sometimes cleaning gives me the illusion that I'm at least making forward progress in one part of my life."

"Nothing that complicated with me. I went to get something and noticed the shelf was sticky. Once I did one shelf it just made sense to do the others. Everything's fine." I gave the syrup spill another swipe with the cleaner.

"Well then, I'll leave you to it." Grandma pushed herself up from the counter and headed off into the living room.

I waited until she was gone and then I sat down on the kitchen counter. I grabbed the postcard off the fridge and flipped it over. My dad had written a quote on the back: *There is no way to peace. Peace is the way.* *A. J. Muste.*

Suddenly I felt tired. Finishing the shelves seemed like entirely too much work. In fact, putting everything back seemed impossible. I fanned myself with the postcard. Maybe Brenda was right— the revenge plan might be the wrong path. Maybe my parents were right with their whole "give peace a chance" thing. Maybe there was such a thing as good enough. Maybe it was time to give it up, to stop worrying about Lauren. I thought every time I pulled something over on her it would feel like a victory, but so far it mostly felt frustrating. And lately it was an annoyance to worry about her at all. Instead of plotting my next scheme for her I could plot to see Christopher again. That had the potential for a pretty good payoff. Perhaps if my life wasn't so complicated, he wouldn't find me to be too much work. I picked up a soup can and rolled it back and forth between my hands. Andy Warhol did a great soup can painting. Brenda would most likely help me pull together an art portfolio if I wanted to try art or design school. I couldn't see myself doing advertising, but maybe something like fabric design. There were a bunch of art schools in Boston, or New York if I felt like going there. I wondered where Christopher was thinking of going for film school. Not that I was planning on stalking him or anything.

I popped off the counter and went back to my room. I would finish in the kitchen later; right now there was something else I needed to clean up. I shut the door to my room and fished my revenge binder back out from under my bed. I flipped through it. I had spent a lot of time on it, but looking at it now it felt like someone else had written it. I held it for a second. I almost felt like crying, but I couldn't have told you why. Then before I could think about it anymore I yanked my life list out and let the rest of it drop into the trash can.

Done. The fate of Lauren was officially in the hands of karma. From now on, I'd just worry about my own.

Chapter Thirty-Six

The next day I couldn't talk to Brenda until rehearsal. She hadn't been in school all afternoon because of a dentist appointment. When I found her she was fiddling with one of the prop doors that kept sticking.

"Hey," I said.

"Do you know what we can do with this? I'm worried I'm going to end up stuck on the wrong side and miss a cue."

"I'll add it to the list for Ms. H." I looked around to see if we were alone. "I wanted to talk to you about something."

"Sure," Brenda said, opening and closing the door, trying to wear it down. "About the door?"

"No, ignore the door for a minute. You were right about the revenge thing. It's time to let it go."

Brenda looked at me for a second and then threw her arms around me as if I had announced that I had discovered a cure for Ebola during the only biology class she missed all year. "That's fantastic. What changed your mind?"

"All right, people, let's take our marks. We've got a lot to get through this afternoon. Let's start at the top of act two," Ms. Herbaut called out, interrupting our discussion. "Brenda? We need you."

Brenda looked at me and then over at the stage.

"Don't worry, I'll tell you all about it later."

Brenda skipped onto the stage and gave me a big smile.

"What is she, your girlfriend?"

I turned around to see Lauren standing there with her trademark smirk.

"She's my friend."

"Brenda Bauer? Brenda the space cadet?" She laughed. "Nice choice."

"Thanks. I thought so," I said. Lauren's face looked pinched like she had been chewing on a movie-size container of Sour Patch Kids. I looked at her and realized I felt nothing. "Excuse me," I said as I stepped past her.

I jumped off the stage on my way to my seat and saw Christopher standing at the back, setting up a video camera. I didn't know if I should say anything to him or act like I didn't see him, but before I could decide he raised a hand in greeting. I walked over.

"I'm doing some shots today of the rehearsal, but I wanted to know when I could meet with you. I haven't interviewed you for my film yet."

"Me?"

"You're part of the show, aren't you?"

"You know what? I am."

"All right. Can I call you later?"

"You bet," I stood there looking at him. I found it impossible not to smile. I was sure it would work out between us now that I had gotten rid of Lauren in the middle. Finally I shook my clipboard. "Time to get down to work," I said as if he were trying to keep me from it.

I sat down and chewed on the end of my pen. In theory I was supposed to be making a list of to-do items for Ms. H., but instead I tried to figure out if I could calculate how close Christopher was behind me without looking around. I was pretty sure Brenda would help me figure out a way to explain to him the whole alternate persona thing, one of the many benefits of having a smart friend. It was time to go back to being Helen. I looked at the script. The scene called for Eliza to pass through the flower market. I wrote down plastic flowers on the top of my list.

"Claire?"

I spun around and realized that Ms. Herbaut must have called my name more than once. She sounded annoyed and everyone was looking at me.

"Claire, can you come down here? I need your help."

I hustled down the aisle to join everyone on the stage. Lauren smirked at me.

"Forget your name?" she asked, and a few people laughed.

"Sorry, I was thinking of something else." I waited for the flush of anger I usually felt when Lauren pulled her condescending act, but I didn't care.

"Can you tape out where everyone is standing at the beginning of the scene?" Ms. Herbaut asked.

"Can you start with me, please?" Lauren asked. "I can't stand here all day, I'm supposed to run through one of the songs again with Rubin." Lauren motioned to the orchestra pit where Rubin was filling in as pianist for practices. He jumped when he heard his name, and I could see his giant Adam's apple bopping up and down.

"I can wait, Lauren," he said, his voice slightly cracking.

"Well, I don't want to wait," she snapped.

I bent down and taped an X on the floor where it met the tip of Lauren's shoe.

"There you go. You're free," I said. Our eyes met and she looked at me slightly confused.

"Actually, Miss Wood, I need to see you briefly," a voice said from the rear of the auditorium. It was Principal LaPoint.

"Me?" Lauren asked, pointing to herself. Everyone in the auditorium looked back and forth between Lauren and Mr. LaPoint. Lauren was not the typical student called into his office.

"Yes. Please bring your bag and come with me."

"I can't go now; we're in the middle of practice."

The vein in Mr. LaPoint's forehead began to pulse. People didn't tell him no very often.

"I've already called your mother. I think it would be better if we had this discussion in my office."

Lauren stomped her foot down. "Can't this wait? I've got to leave here and go straight to cheerleading. What's the big deal?"

"Miss Wood, I think we should discuss this in my office."

"Discuss what?"

"You've been accused of possessing drugs, Miss Wood," Mr. LaPoint spat out. My stomach fell into my shoes. Oh shit. This wasn't supposed to happen. If Mr. LaPoint had been expecting Lauren to cower in fright, he was wrong. She looked at him and laughed. Of course she had no idea what was coming. I didn't feel like laughing at all.

"You're joking," she said.

"I'm not joking. Now, if you will come with me."

"I don't do drugs," Lauren said with a toss of her hair.

"Then you don't mind if I search your bag?"

"No."

"Lauren, maybe you should wait until your mom gets here," Ms. Herbaut said.

"It's no big deal. This is obviously a mistake."

Lauren jumped off the stage and walked to the side of the auditorium where everyone had dumped their bags and coats on the floor. She pulled out her giant black leather tote. I wanted to stop what I knew was going to happen, but short of pulling a fire alarm I couldn't think of anything to do.

"If you look through my bag, then I'm free to go, right?" She handed Mr. LaPoint her tote and tossed her hair. "I'm assuming a strip search won't be required."

Someone in the front rows snickered and Mr. LaPoint looked over, his gaze freezing everyone into silence. He walked over to the table at the front and placed the bag down as if he were about to start a tricky medical procedure. He unzipped various pockets and stacked Lauren's things on the table: pens, three different shades of lipstick, a small notebook, her iPod, a roll of wintergreen Life Savers, some nail polish, a stack of Kleenex folded into fours.

Lauren stood watching him, her hip cocked out to the side looking bored. The rest of the cast and crew didn't even pretend to ignore what was going on. They jockeyed for position to see what would happen. I could see Brenda standing near the back, and she looked as nervous as if she were the one in trouble instead of Lauren.

"Satisfied?" Lauren asked in a voice that implied she would have her daddy's lawyer down to the school first thing in the morning to bring charges against Mr. LaPoint.

For a second I thought it might work out okay, that he wouldn't see it. That however this had gotten screwed up would work itself back out. Then he found it, buried deep in the front pocket: a tin of Altoids. He popped the tin open and then smiled. Lauren's brow furrowed. He turned the tin and there, nestled in the paper were two joints.

The cast and crew let out an appreciative *ooh* for a trick well done. The blood dropped out of Lauren's face. I felt like I wanted to throw up.

"That isn't mine," she said.

"That's what I tell my folks too when they catch me!" yelled out one of the guys in the chorus, and everyone started laughing.

"Miss Wood, if you'll come with me." Mr. LaPoint reached for her elbow and she yanked it away. Lauren's lower lip started to shake. Any drug offenses were an automatic dismissal from the cheerleading squad. Not to mention what her mom and dad were going to say. I froze when I saw Brenda. She was looking at me in shock.

"They're not mine," Lauren said again, even louder.

Mr. LaPoint reached for her again, this time taking her by the forearm. Once he had a hold on her she crumpled. It was like every bone in her body turned to water and she collapsed to the floor.

"NO!" She yelled out. Ms. Herbaut stood up and moved forward, but it was clear she didn't know what to do.

"Please come with me, Miss Wood," Mr. LaPoint repeated.

Lauren didn't say anything. She just began to cry. Mr. LaPoint took her elbow and lifted her to her feet. He half carried and half led her out of the auditorium, her handbag stuffed under his arm. He gave Ms. Herbaut a stiff nod as he walked out the door. The room erupted with everyone talking to everyone else.

I turned around and realized that Christopher had caught the whole thing on film.

"Okay, everyone quiet down," Ms. Herbaut said, raising her

voice over the din. "Everyone give it a rest. We're going to move on with practice." She flipped through the script at random. "Casey, let's run through your scene."

Casey, a shy-looking sophomore, went on stage while everyone else dropped their voices back down to a murmur.

"I can honestly say I didn't see that coming," Ms. Herbaut whispered to me.

Brenda was standing at the edge of the stage looking at me. She shook her head before turning around and walking away.

"Me neither," I mumbled. This was only half true. I can't say it was totally unexpected. I knew how the joints got in her purse; I'd put them there a few days ago during lunch. The question was, who called Mr. LaPoint and turned her in?

Chapter Thirty-Seven

J grabbed my jacket out of my locker. My mind kept replaying the situation over and over. No one could focus after the drug drama, so we ended rehearsal early, and the halls were already empty. Most of the students and teachers had gone home. I could hear people in the student newspaper office. I wondered if they would consider this a breaking story. The janitor was waxing up the floors, and the hum of the machine bounced off the tile floors and cement walls.

I shut the locker door and Brenda was standing there. I stepped back.

"Whoa, way to sneak up on people," I said.

Brenda didn't even crack a smile. "What are you going to do?"

"About what?"

"About what happened." Brenda looked to see if anyone was around and lowered her voice. "You were the one who put those in her bag, weren't you?"

"Yes."

"Where did you get the pot?" Brenda's head kept whipping back and forth as if the vice squad might swoop down on us at any moment.

"I asked Tyler from my gym class."

"And he just gave it to you?" Brenda looked appalled.

"Well, he made me pay for it. It wasn't like a charity thing or anything."

"What happened to giving up the revenge plan? You couldn't resist one last chance to get her back?"

"I did give up the plan. I stuck the stuff in her purse a while ago, but I swear I didn't call LaPoint. I'd been planning to make an anonymous tip to the cheerleading coach, but that was before we talked and I decided to dump the whole revenge plan. I never told anyone."

"The cheerleading coach? Why?"

"So Lauren would be kicked off the squad. They have a zero tolerance policy. Cheerleading was the only item that I hadn't checked off."

"Well, you wouldn't want to leave anything unchecked."

"I keep telling you, I'm done with all that," I said, throwing my arms up in the air. "Someone else called LaPoint." I was practically yelling at this point and I noticed that the janitor had turned off the floor buffer and was watching us like our little drama was better than cable TV. I gave him a smile and pulled Brenda down the hall. We went outside and stood by the door.

"I didn't plan for this to happen," I said. Brenda gave a snort. "Okay, I planned it, but I gave up the plan. I don't know who did this today. Maybe someone else saw a chance to get her back. Who knows, maybe karma finally caught up to her."

I shuffled in place. I'd waited a long time for Lauren's downfall. I'd dreamed about it for years. Now that it finally happened it didn't feel nearly as good as I'd anticipated. Especially with the way Brenda was looking at me.

Brenda's mom pulled into the parking lot and flashed her lights.

Brenda shook her head at me, then jogged over to the car and got in. I waved as they drove away, hoping it would infuse Brenda with confidence that somehow things would work out for the best.

So much for victory being sweet.

Chapter Thirty-Eight

The door to the school slammed open, and I jumped back out of the way. Mrs. Wood stormed down the stairs, dragging Lauren behind her. Neither of them saw me. I was afraid to move and draw attention to myself.

"Never in my life have I been so humiliated," Mrs. Wood said. It was clear to see where Lauren's nostril-flaring talent came from: Her mom's nostrils were wide enough to comfortably hold a tennis ball in each.

"It wasn't mine. I'm telling you, someone planted it there," Lauren said. Her face was red and blotchy.

Mrs. Wood spun around and Lauren pulled back as if she thought her mom would hit her. Mrs. Wood yanked Lauren closer by her wrist so that she could yell directly in her face.

"I don't care if it's yours. What I care about is that you are dragging the name of this family through the muck. You better believe that there are plenty of people in this town who would love the chance to tear down your father and me, and you just gave them a way to do it."

"But it isn't true."

"I don't care about the truth, Lauren. I care about how it looks. I care about what people think is the truth. You know, I don't ask that much of you, just that you stay at the top of your game, that you represent this family to the best of your ability, and you can't even do that."

Mrs. Wood shook her head in disgust and stomped toward the street.

"Mom, I'm scared," Lauren said in a wobbling voice. She was still frozen on the stairs.

Mrs. Wood spun back around. "Well, Lauren, frankly I don't care what you feel. What we need to focus on is how we're going to fix this. Your father is going to get a lawyer and you're going to do whatever we need you to do to make this situation go away. You can save your tears for some other time and place." Lauren's mom yanked open the door to her Lexus SUV, her diamond bracelets winking in the sunlight. "Move it," she said, getting in and slamming the door behind her.

Lauren's shoulders slumped over and she walked slowly to the car. Her mom sat in the driver's seat staring straight ahead. When Lauren got to the car she looked up and saw me standing by the side of the school door. I saw her chest hitch and she started crying harder. She opened the door and crawled into the SUV and her mom tore off before she had finished closing the door.

"I'm sorry," I said, but no one was there to hear it.

Chapter Thirty-Nine

There is no doubt in my mind that I have the strangest parents in the world. They wear only all-natural fibers and actually like the taste of tofu tacos. They've dragged me to all kinds of weird self-exploration workshops where I learned to meditate, chant, rub crystals, and burn sage stalks to smudge the evil spirits from my life. I'm pretty sure both of them think they have been through previous lives. They're weird, but they love me. They love who I am, not what or who they wanted me to be or thought I could be. They want me to be happy. I knew without a doubt that if the situation had been reversed, if I were in Lauren's shoes, they would want to know the truth and they would stay with me until we figured it out together.

It was possible that the worst thing in the world wasn't being betrayed by your so-called best friend; maybe the worst thing was being betrayed by your family.

Lauren wasn't in school the next day and there wasn't a soul in all of Lincoln High who didn't know why. A couple of geeky juniors who had been on the receiving end of some of Lauren's cruel comments over the years spit on her locker as they walked past, and someone else had written BITCH on it in marker. It was clear that while Lauren might have been popular, that wasn't the same thing as being well liked.

Bailey, Kyla, and the rest of the cheerleading squad were warming up for a lunchtime practice. Apparently there was some big cheerleading derby or something coming up that called for extra practices. Bailey had asked me to come for moral support, so I sat on the slick gym floor watching and picking at my sandwich.

"Hey, can you give a message to Lauren for me?" One of the guys from the football team said as he jogged past.

Kyla gave a curt nod.

"Tell her if she's looking for blow, she don't need to do drugs. She can have this." He grabbed his crotch and gave it a shake. The rest of the guys burst out laughing.

"That was disgusting," Bailey said, looking away and pulling her leg effortlessly up above her head in a stretch. "I still can't believe the whole thing."

"It's not like it's the first time she did something without thinking," Kyla pointed out.

"True, but I don't think she did it," I said. "I think someone stuck that stuff in her bag for LaPoint to find."

"That's terrible. Who would do that to Lauren?" Bailey asked.

"That's what we need to figure out," I said.

"Now we're going to be Nancy Drew?" Kyla asked with a laugh. I had a sudden flash of Lauren cutting her palm so we would be in trouble together after our Nancy Drew adventure had gone bad.

"Yeah, now we play Nancy Drew. We figure out a way to clear Lauren's name."

"I feel terrible about what happened, but I don't want to get messed up in the situation." Kyla bent over, bouncing as she touched her toes. She looked back at me. "What? I've got my cheerleading slot to think about. Anyone mixed up in drugs is an auto off the squad. Who knows what happened? Maybe she was holding them for someone. Maybe they *are* hers. At the party last week she took a toke off someone's joint. She's no angel."

"Smoking that stuff is wrong." Bailey's mouth pressed into a thin line. Clearly Mary Poppins did not approve of recreational weed. "You start with marijuana and then it leads to heavier stuff. She could have ruined her life."

Kyla rolled her eyes. "Don't freak out, Miss Just Say No. She got caught with two joints. It isn't like she was shooting heroin. The whole thing is no big deal. Her cheerleading days are over, but Daddy's lawyer will keep her out of any real trouble."

I looked over at Bailey and she looked away, pulling at her pleated skirt.

"It isn't that I don't want to help Lauren. It's just, my parents told me I'm not allowed to hang out with her anymore. They're like superstrict and stuff," Bailey said.

The cheerleading coach blew her whistle and motioned that she wanted everyone to join her in the center of the gym floor. I stood up and chucked the rest of my sandwich into the trash.

"I don't know why you want to help Lauren so bad. You know she totally talks shit about you," Kyla said. "You might think she's your friend, but she's not. Lauren hates competition, and as far as she's concerned, you never knew your place."

"She never said anything that bad," Bailey said, clearly feeling awkward. "Lauren just gets sort of short sometimes. She hates change."

"Whatever," Kyla muttered, doing a few last twists at the waist. "I wouldn't worry about her. Things have a way of working out for Lauren." Kyla ran off with her skirt flipping up.

"It'll be okay. I think it's super nice you want to help her out, but maybe she needed to get caught to keep herself from getting into even deeper trouble. It might have been the best thing that could have happened to her." Bailey gave my arm a soft rub.

Oh no. She didn't.

"Bailey, did you turn in Lauren?"

She pulled back. I could read her like an open book. She was thinking of lying, but she didn't have the slightest idea how to do it. Dishonesty wasn't something that came easy to her.

"It isn't that I wanted her to get in trouble." Her eyes filled with tears. "Real friends do what's right, even when it feels wrong."

I sank down to the floor. Lauren was taken down by Mary Poppins. Bailey kneeled in front of me on the floor. "What happened?" I asked.

"I went in her purse to get a mint and I found the drugs." Bailey twisted her hands together. "Lauren was never into that stuff before, but she's been all weird and tense lately. I've been worried about her. I think she's getting on the wrong track."

"So you turned her in to LaPoint?" I glanced around to see if anyone else was paying attention to our discussion.

"I prayed about it first. I wanted to do the right thing. Now she can get the help she needs." Bailey's lower lip was shaking. "Are you going to tell her it was me?"

My mind was whizzing around like a salad spinner. "No. I won't tell her."

"I really did do it because I care about her."

"I know you did." The coach blew her whistle again. "You better go." Bailey squeezed my hand and then ran over to join the rest of the squad. I clamored up to my feet, brushing off my jeans.

I wasn't sure how she did it, but Lauren had found herself a true friend. I wanted another option, but I couldn't think of one. It wasn't about doing it to help Lauren; it was about doing it because the person I wanted to be would do the right thing. If I was going to get a life, it should be one worth having.

Chapter Forty

I sat outside LaPoint's office, my knees bouncing up and down. I had to think that waiting to tell was going to be worse than the actual telling, but the way the secretary kept shooting looks over at me like my days were numbered made me wonder. I had the sense no one who met with LaPoint got out alive. I had never been in trouble like this before. I wasn't sure what the process would be. Would LaPoint call my grandma? Would they kick me out of school?

Suspension might not be a bad thing. There was no telling how it would go once the rest of the school found out what I did. They might love me for taking down Lauren, but more likely they'd think I was a freaky stalker psycho who lied about everything. Maybe Grandma would be willing to homeschool me for the rest of the year so I could graduate. Then again, once my grandma found out I had lied to her about the revenge plan there was the very serious possibility that she wouldn't feel like doing me any favors.

The door to LaPoint's office swung open and he stood there like a leering Count Dracula. The secretary didn't say a word; she just pointed at me. I felt like doom-and-gloom music should start playing, but the only sound was my pounding heart. I stood up and tried to ignore the fact that every square inch of my body was sweating like I had run a marathon. I walked past Mr. LaPoint and sat in the chair across from his desk.

Mr. LaPoint's office was done in an early prison warden–style, stark and cold. He wasn't the kind of guy to have a lot of knickknacks and mementos hanging around. There was one framed picture on his desk, but it looked like the fake-family shot that came with the frame. I didn't notice any torture devices, like thumbscrews, but I supposed those weren't the kind of thing you'd leave laying around. I nibbled on the skin next to my thumbnail, but when I saw him looking at me I pulled it out of my mouth and sat on both of my hands. I waited for him to say anything, but he just sat there at his desk, his hands folded in front of him on the desk blotter.

"So . . . ," I said, my voice trailing off, but he still sat there silently. I wanted to look at my watch. It felt like I had been sitting there for an hour at least even though I knew it had been a couple minutes at best. Apparently Mr. LaPoint didn't subscribe to the "how to make things easier on you" school of discipline.

"I came to confess something," I said finally.

"Go on."

"I put the joints in Lauren Wood's bag."

"I see."

When I'd thought of how this situation might go, Mr. LaPoint simply saying "I see" hadn't been one of the possible outcomes I had imagined.

"So, I guess you'll clear Lauren's name. I don't know if you need to call my grandma to pick me up or not."

"I don't think that will be necessary."

"Okay." I waited for something to happen. I'd pictured Mr. LaPoint to be more of a yeller. I thought he was going to try to get out of me where I'd gotten the drugs or pull my fingernails out until I confessed my secret identity. Nothing. He sat there with his hands folded on the desk, looking at me. "Where do we go from here?" I asked.

"You go back to class, Miss Dantes." He pushed back from the desk and stood.

"Class?" Was that a joke? Would I go to open the door and find myself taken down by a taser?

"While I appreciate the sentiment, lying isn't tolerated here."

"What?"

Mr. LaPoint gave a chuckle. "You're friends with Miss Wood, aren't you? You hang with her little crowd."

Little crowd? How patronizing could this guy be? "Lauren and I aren't friends."

"Ah, perhaps you're hoping if you take the heat for this situation she'll be endlessly grateful. I know how young girls can be;

I've been doing this job for a long time. Cliques can be difficult to manage, especially for someone new. I don't know if she put you up to it or if you took it upon yourself, but either way, it doesn't matter."

"I put the drugs in there," I insisted again, as if repeating the information would somehow help. How could he not believe me?

"I know you're involved in the theater program, Miss Dantes, but allow me to remind you that drama should stay on the stage. I will refrain from granting you a detention this time, but I trust that your"—he made finger quotations in the air—"'confession' will be your last such attention-getting scheme." Mr. LaPoint strode to the door and opened it. "I have confidence this is the last time we'll have this discussion."

I trudged past him and he shut the door behind me. I held my hands out and they were shaking. If I pushed Lauren to the very edge of a cliff, did it really matter that she took the last step herself? I would feel just as guilty as I would if I had shoved her. If you try to do the right thing and no one believes you, does it still count?

Chapter Forty-One

$\mathcal{I}$ told the secretary I was sick. She took one look at me and decided I wasn't lying. I wasn't. It wasn't the flu, but I had a serious case of guilt-induced stomach upset that made the whole strawberry to the handbag incident look minor. The idea of sitting in class and acting like everything was fine seemed impossible.

Grandma wasn't home when I got there. I walked around the house. I didn't want to lie down and couldn't think of anything that I wanted to do. I clicked on the TV and flipped through the afternoon court TV shows. I tried to get interested in who got justice, but it seemed too complicated to follow. When Judge Judy starts being too complex you have to know you aren't at your best. The Turner movie channel was showing *What Ever Happened to Baby Jane?* Even a creepy Bette Davis movie wasn't going to do the trick.

I picked up the phone and put it down. Then I saw the

number stuck to the fridge with a magnet. I pulled it off and dialed it without thinking about it any more. The receptionist at the meditation camp went to get my mom.

"Hey, Poppet, is everything okay?" As soon as I heard my mom's voice, I felt better. I clutched the phone close to my face as if that would bring us closer together.

"I hope I didn't interrupt you from reaching enlightenment or anything."

"You're never an interruption."

"Mom, how to do you fix karma?"

"Karma isn't a broken thing."

"What if someone did something, say, a bad something, but when they did it they knew it was wrong, but thought they were doing it for the right reason, but then they realized it wasn't the right reason, but the situation was already out of control and then everything was all screwed up?" The words flew out of me in a giant run-on sentence.

"Well, assuming I followed that last bit, I guess I would tell this mysterious someone that everything we do and say has an impact on the world around us. If this person has put something out in the world that was wrong, then she needs to double her efforts to put in something good."

"Sort of balance things out," I said, with a sniff.

"Exactly."

"What if she tried to make things right, but it didn't work?"

"What do you do when you draw something and it doesn't come out right?"

"I erase it and do it over."

"There you are. We need to redraw the world when we don't like what's in front of us."

I could hear the chime of a bell in the background. "I suppose I should let you go," I said.

"I can stay and talk longer if you want."

"No. I'm okay. Will you tell Dad I said hi?"

"Of course. One more thing: Karma is a heavy weight. Hard to move, hard to change."

"Yeah, I'm getting that idea."

"That's why it's always best to get a helping hand. You can leverage so much more when you don't do it alone."

I hung up the phone and then picked it up again before I could talk myself out it. Brenda picked up on the second ring.

"I need your help," I blurted. "All those times I was giving you advice? You were right, I should have been taking it from you instead. You're clearly the smart one in this relationship. I'll say I'm sorry a million times in a row, but you have to help me."

"Anyone ever tell you that you're sort of intense?"

"So if I say I'm sorry, say, a hundred times in a row that would cover it?"

"Maybe." I could hear a thaw in Brenda's voice.

"The thing is, the person who turned in Lauren actually did it for the right reason. I don't want to get that person in trouble, but I need to make things right somehow."

"And you think I'll know how to sort this out?"

"I'm pretty much counting on it."

Brenda sighed. "Okay, this is a bit outside my usual area of expertise, but in science if you screw up, the honorable thing to do is make it public. You write a paper about where you went off track and publish it where all your colleagues will see it. You have to own the error."

"You think I should take out an ad in the school paper saying I planted the drugs?"

"I'm not saying it's the best plan, but it is an option. Do you have any other ideas?"

"Not really. Science isn't my thing."

"What's your thing?"

"Movies."

"What do they do in the movies?"

"In the movies when a character wants to redeem himself, he has to make a noble sacrifice. Like when Rhett Butler leaves Scarlett O'Hara in the middle of the invasion of Atlanta to join the army, even though he knows they'll lose."

"I think joining the army and heading off to war to your certain doom is going a bit far."

"Yeah, I look lousy in a uniform. I can sacrifice something though." I picked up a pen sitting by the phone and tapped it on the counter. "I'm going to have to kill off Claire."

"At least she'll die with a purpose." Leave it to Brenda to find a silver lining.

"Before I put her obituary in the paper there's someone I need to talk to." My voice shook slightly.

"What do you think he'll say?"

"I don't know. I might end up sacrificing a chance with him too."

"Or it might make a chance possible."

Chapter Forty-Two

I got to the theater early, but Christopher was already there. He was sitting near the back with his eyes closed while he waited for the show to start. They were showing *Flying Leathernecks*. I took a deep breath and moved down the aisle. He opened his eyes when I sat down. I motioned to the pile of junk food in his lap—a bucket of buttered popcorn, a giant box of Junior Mints, and a bag of those SweeTart knockoffs that taste like sour sugar cubes.

"Hungry?" I asked.

"Dinner of champions." He shook the popcorn in my direction and I took a handful. "I take it you've decided you like old movies?"

"I think I always did." I took a deep breath. "I need to talk to you."

"Now?" He looked confused. Talking and movies don't usually go together. The lights went down and the Dolby sound kicked into overdrive. It was so loud, the sound waves pushed me back into the chair. The previews were apparently being screened for those with hearing impairments.

"No, it can wait." I wasn't sure what he was going to do when I told him the truth. He might be Lincoln High's bad boy, but he had his own clearly defined sense of right and wrong.

"I'm glad you came," he said, before scrunching down in his seat.

"Me too," I whispered, but I wasn't sure he heard me.

"How can you not like John Wayne?" Christopher asked as we walked out to our cars after the movie. "It's like saying you don't like baseball or apple pie. It's un-American."

"It's not exactly the same as flag burning or marching for anarchy."

"It might be worse. What about his film *Fort Apache*?"

"Nope."

"Okay, *Rio Grande*?"

"Meh." I waved my hand back and forth.

"*Hellfighters*?"

I gave a shrug. "*The Quiet Man* was okay."

"Oscar-winning film and she says it was okay."

"You know what happened to Lauren? Those drugs weren't hers." I said it in a rush, before I lost my nerve.

"Holy changing topics, Batman," he said.

"No, I'm being serious. I know they weren't hers."

"Why do you always bring her up?"

"I don't always bring her up," I protested.

Christopher gave a laugh, which ticked me off for some reason.

"I don't bring her up that often," I said, trying to calm my voice.

"Hey, don't get mad. You can talk about whoever you want. Everyone else is talking about her these days."

"That's what I'm trying to talk to you about."

"Now listen here, pilgrim, you don't want to get involved with the law, " he said with a really bad imitation of John Wayne. I crossed my arms across my chest. "Oops, that's right. I forgot you hated him. Look, you're right. The stuff wasn't Lauren's."

I suddenly felt light-headed. "How do you know?"

"That girl is wound way too tight to be smoking weed on a regular basis. I mean ask yourself, does she strike you as someone that people would call mellow?" he asked.

My mouth clicked shut. The logic there was hard to ignore.

"I put the stuff in her purse."

"Why would you do that?" He took a step back. I had to fight the urge to step closer.

"This is a long story. Is there some place we could talk?"

Chapter Forty-Three

Christopher had a tree house. It was built high in a giant oak tree in the woods that ran behind his neighborhood. He jumped up to pull down a rope ladder and motioned that I should climb up first. I hadn't been in a tree house since I was ten, but this was about a thousand times better than any tree house I had ever seen. The floor was straight and felt solid. The roof was large, shingled with a generous overhang. The walls went up only half way so you could look out between the branches. It felt more like an outpost than a tree house.

Christopher climbed up behind me. There was a giant Rubbermaid container in the corner, and he popped it open to pull out some blankets. He spread one on the floor and then passed me a worn blue fleece blanket.

"It's getting cold," he said. He pulled another blanket out for himself and then a lantern, which he fired up. It gave the space a sort of yellow glow. If we'd had some marshmallows and a fire it would feel like camp. Of course I suspected Smokey the bear frowns on campfires being set in trees, given that they are flammable and all.

"Nice place," I said, breaking the silence.

"It's a little elementary school, which is fair since it's been mine since elementary school, but you wanted a place we could be alone. This would be it."

"You make it yourself?"

"Me? No. My dad and I built it when I was a kid. He knew how to make stuff last, but he wasn't as good with keeping relationships going. This tree house will be around for years, which is more than I could say for him."

"I'm sorry."

"Don't be. I got over feeling bad about that a few years ago. All my family trauma will give me something to talk about when I'm interviewed as a famous director. Gotta have something to fill up those behind-the-scenes DVD sections. And if nothing else, this gives me a place to go when my mom and I aren't getting along. I like to think of it as my dad's lovely parting gift."

I pulled the blanket around me so I was wrapped up like a fleece burrito. I took a deep breath and began at the beginning. "When you said things with me were complicated you were right. You know how my grandma calls me Helen? Well . . ."

Christopher didn't interrupt while I told the whole story. I wasn't sure what he thought, but I was considering it a positive that he didn't get up and leave.

"That's it," I said, in case he hadn't guessed from the silence that the story was over.

"Can't say I expected that."

"The thing is, I didn't call LaPoint." I felt it was important that he knew that I hadn't done this final piece of damage.

"But you would have. I mean, maybe not LaPoint, but you would have gotten her in trouble at some point. Your point was to destroy her, wasn't it?"

I pulled at the thread on the edge of the blanket. "Yes." A tear ran down my face, it felt hot on my cheek. That was the first time I realized how cold the night had gotten. "I'm sorry that I did it. I'm sorry that it ended up hurting Lauren, and I'm sorry that I lied to you and Brenda. I always thought that Lauren ruined everything for me, but the truth is, the reason I never made any other real friends is because I'm lousy at it."

"I'm pretty lousy at the people thing too."

"You're better than me."

"Take this in the nicest way, but you haven't exactly set the bar real high."

It was hard to argue with that. I pulled the blanket closer. "The whole thing will come out tomorrow after school."

"Should make for an interesting day."

"Can you forgive me?" I held my breath waiting for him to answer.

"How can I forgive you? I don't really know who you are."

Do not cry. Do not cry. I reminded myself that you didn't see

Rhett Butler crying. You can't be noble and a crybaby at the same time. Tomorrow was another day and all that. "Fair enough."

I stood up and folded the blanket. I passed it back to Christopher without saying anything else and crawled down the rope ladder. I jumped down the last few feet.

"Hey, Helen." Christopher poked his head out of the tree house. I could hardly make out his features in the dark. "I don't know who you are, but it might be interesting to find out," he said.

My face burst into a huge smile. "I can promise you, with me it will almost certainly be interesting."

Chapter Forty-Four

I left school early. I didn't want to be around when they distributed the paper with my CLAIRE DANTES=HELEN WORTHINGTON ad in it at the end of the day. Besides, there was one other person I had to talk to. Lauren's mom answered the door. She was wearing slacks that looked freshly ironed and a scarf tied at her waist like a belt, an expensive, all-silk belt. I wondered if she stood up all day to avoid being wrinkled. The dark circles under her eyes were the only things out of place. Otherwise she looked perfect. She didn't say anything; she simply raised one eyebrow as a question. I guessed my paint-stained yoga pants weren't kicking her hospitality gene into action.

"Is Lauren home?" I held up the tote bag full of books I had brought. "I go to school with her. I have all her homework and stuff."

"I'll see that she gets it." Mrs. Wood held out one perfectly manicured hand.

"I sort of need to see her. Some of it has to be explained."

Mrs. Wood didn't say anything else but led the way. I followed after her, past the designer kitchen that looked as if it had never been used, through the living room with its uncomfortably stiff furniture, and up the stairs. She tapped on the door to Lauren's bedroom with her fingernail and walked away.

"Come in," Lauren said.

I pushed open the door. Lauren was propped up in bed; she had the TV on showing a rerun of *Gossip Girl*. When she saw me she clicked it off. She sat up straighter and ran her fingers through her hair, which looked a bit grimy. I had felt panicky on the way over, but for some reason, now that I was in the middle of everything, I felt strangely calm.

"I brought you a bunch of stuff from school."

If I had been waiting for her to say thanks, then it looked like it was going to be a long wait.

"Are you feeling okay?" I asked.

"I'm fine."

The conversation seemed to have run out of steam again.

"Did you want anything else?" Lauren asked.

"I came to say I'm sorry."

"For what?"

"Remember when you said you started having all kinds of bad luck when I showed up? That wasn't all by accident."

"Did you do this too? Did you stick that stuff in my purse?"

"Yes." From the look in Lauren's eye I could tell she was already planning to sic her daddy's lawyer on me like a pit bull. "I suppose you want to know why I did this?" I said.

"No, *Helen*, I know exactly why you did it."

I backed up until I hit the wall. "How long have you known?"

"I suspected for a while. I didn't know for sure until now. Did you really think you could keep it a secret forever? I *know* you. I know you better than anyone. I would have guessed even sooner except I didn't think anyone could be that twisted." Lauren got off the bed and walked across the room. She crossed her arms and looked at me. "I bet you're really proud of yourself, huh?"

"Not really."

"I doubt that."

"I came to say I'm sorry."

"You should be." Lauren stepped closer so that our faces were inches apart. "Is this where you expect me to say I'm sorry too? To throw myself to the floor and beg you to forgive me? Maybe we could sit down and talk it all over and end up swearing to be best friends forever? Maybe your mom and dad could make a peace circle out in the woods and we could dance by the moonlight in some weird pagan ritual."

"I don't expect us to be friends, but you know we used to be. There was a time when I would have done anything for you."

"That was your problem, not mine."

"You're right. It just took me a longer time to catch on than it should have. Friendship is supposed to go both ways."

"Wow, that's deep. You should make up T-shirts or something."

"I came to tell you I'm sorry. What you did to me was wrong; what I did was wrong too. It's even now. We're done."

"What if I say it's not done? What if I have my dad get his lawyer and sue your family for every stupid trinket they own? You do own some things, don't you? What do you think the kids at school are going to say when this comes out? You think they're going to like you, knowing that you basically came here to stalk me? Why don't you just admit you want to be me? This was all about trying to steal my life because you're jealous."

"I've been confused about a lot of stuff, but the one thing I'm certain of is I never want to be you." But I realized as I said it that she was almost right. In getting the revenge, I almost turned into her, and that would have been the worst outcome I could imagine.

"Whatever. We'll see what everyone has to say."

"The people who matter to me already know who I am. As for telling everyone else, you don't need to worry. I'm guessing it's public knowledge by now." I put the bag of books down on the floor and turned to leave. That's when I saw them. How could I have missed that when I had been in her room last time? I walked across the room and ran my fingers across one of her bookshelves, along her collection of hardcover Nancy Drew mysteries.

I picked one up and flipped through the pages. Stuffed in the back were our detective agency business cards and some pictures of the two of us together. I smiled when I saw one of the photos. It was a sleepover. I don't remember the occasion, but my folks had allowed us to pretend we were pioneers. They'd turned the heat down in the house and we had slept in front of the fireplace. In the morning my mom had made pancakes, and we had drowned them in a lake of maple syrup. The photo was of the two of us sitting in front of the fireplace with our plates balanced in our laps. I could remember everything about that moment. The way the smoke of the fire mixed with the smell of pancakes and how I ended up with sticky syrup in my hair. We had laughed so much that night I couldn't even remember if we ever went to sleep. I flipped the photo over so she could see it.

Lauren's lower lip was shaking.

"We had some good times," I said softly. Lauren shrugged. She wouldn't look me directly in the eye. "You take care of yourself, Lauren Wood."

Chapter Forty-Five

I slipped out of Lauren's room and down the stairs. I let myself out the door without saying good-bye to Mrs. Wood. I didn't owe her anything.

I heard a honk and looked up. Christopher's car was parked across the street. He and Brenda got out. I felt a smile break out across my face.

"How did it go?" Brenda asked.

"I don't think she and I are going to be best friends, if that's what you're asking."

"Of course not, I'm your best friend. The position is already taken," Brenda said.

"What are you guys doing here?"

"If you can believe it, she just admitted she's never seen an Audrey Hepburn movie," Christopher said, motioning to Brenda.

"What? I told you to watch those weeks ago," I said.

"Things got a bit busy."

"We've rented the whole series: *Sabrina, Breakfast at Tiffany's,* and of course, *My Fair Lady*." Christopher counted them off on his fingers. "We're going over to her place to order pizza."

"And you came to get me?"

"How can I get to know you unless we spend time together?" Christopher leaned over and kissed the corner of my mouth. "Besides, Brenda tells me you've got only one night before you're doomed to be grounded. I thought I better see you while I still had the chance."

"Good point. Lockdown begins tomorrow. If Lauren gets my parents involved there may even be forced community service hours."

"Don't worry. In addition to heist movies, I've seen a lot of prison break movies. There's hope for you yet."

I was almost afraid to ask, but I had to know.

"So what was the response to my ad?"

"I think you should look at transferring schools," Brenda said. My mouth fell open and she burst out laughing. "I'm joking."

"Most people I heard talking about it thought the whole thing was sort of cool," Christopher said. "Who knows, maybe it will make you even more popular."

"I don't care about being popular anymore. Well, except with the present company."

We piled into Christopher's car. While Brenda and Christopher debated the merits of different pizza toppings, I flipped through the DVD movie cases they had picked up.

Old movies are black-and-white; they've got good guys and bad guys. The thing was, I didn't want to live in the past anymore. It was time for my life to go full color.

Acknowledgments

When I buy a book I always read the acknowledgments section. I think I'm hoping to see my name in it. In that spirit, my first thanks go to you for picking this book to read. Feel free to pencil your name in here. You deserve it.

Big thanks to my friends and family who put up with me. At times this is harder than you might think. You can't choose your family, but if I could, I would choose the one I have. As for my friends, I couldn't imagine better, and that is saying something because I make stuff up for a living.

One of the best parts of writing has been the support and friendship of other writers. For all the help with brainstorming, talking me off the ledge, and inspiring me with your writing, thanks go to Joelle Anthony, Allison Pritchard, Robyn Harding, Shanna Mahin, Carol Mason, Nancy Warren, Eileen Rendahl, Serena Robar, Carolyn Rapanos, Meg Cabot, everyone connected to the Debutante Ball, Joanne Levy, Brooke Chapman, Lani Diane Rich, Jen Lancaster, Allison Winn Scotch, Alison Pace, and Barrie Summy. A special nod to Dumas, who wrote *The Count of Monte Cristo*, the inspiration for this book.

My agent, Rachel Vater, continues to be both a great business partner and friend. Thanks for all your guidance, support, and late night discussions on skeptical topics. Huge thanks to my editor, Anica Mrose Rissi, who shares my love of good books, good food, and dogs, even when they're being bad. Your feedback is wonderful and makes each book better. I'd write books with you anytime. The entire team at Simon Pulse is fantastic. Special thanks go to Cara Petrus, who designs covers that are so wonderful I want to lick them.

Special thanks to my husband, Bob, who always believed this was possible. You are my happy ending. My two dogs deserve thanks for providing me with disgusting half-chewed toys as a distraction. It's like having a live action Cute Overload in the house.

Lastly a huge thanks to my readers. There are so many good books to choose from, I appreciate people giving mine a chance. Please be sure to drop by my website and let me know what you think of the book. I'd love to hear from you! www.eileencook.com

Don't miss

THE EDUCATION OF HAILEY KENDRICK

by Eileen Cook.

Here's an exclusive first look.

There was a matter of life and death to deal with, and instead we were wasting our time discussing Mandy Gallaway's crotch. I kept a neutral smile plastered on my face, but my foot bobbed up and down impatiently. More people have seen Mandy Gallaway's naked crotch than saw last year's Super Bowl. The girl's incapable of getting out of a car without flashing the sixty zillion paparazzi that follow her around. The concept of knees together and underwear on isn't that complicated, which leaves me to believe she likes the sensation of flashbulbs lighting up where the sun isn't supposed to shine.

Given that her crotch had been photographed more than most supermodels, I failed to see why one online leaked picture of her standing in her gym shorts and a sports bra was causing this much drama. The situation certainly didn't call for the public flogging and stoning the student body was advocating. All the crowd was missing were some pitchforks and torches, and we could have stormed the town. On the upside, at least people had shown up for our student government meeting, for a change.

The Evesham student body usually had more important things to care about, like planning their next vacation to a private island near the Bahamas, or deciding between another Coach or Louis Vuitton bag. Most of the time the only people who came to our meetings were those of us on the board.

It wasn't clear what had really happened, but the theory was that a female security guard had snapped the photo of the half-dressed Mandy in the locker room and had sold it to the tabloids. A few people had seen a guard doing her rounds of the gym, and she'd had her cell phone out. Given who attends Evesham, paparazzi is a common problem, but before this incident they'd tended to hang outside the school gates. No one had ever had a picture leaked from inside. This was officially big news on campus.

"We should send her to prison for violating Mandy's privacy," Garrett said. His dad is a U.S. Senator; you would think he would have a better idea of how the system works.

"We're a student government association," I pointed out. "We don't actually have the power to sentence anyone to jail time." I straightened the nameplate on the desk in front of me: HAILEY KENDRICK, VICE PRESIDENT. I managed to avoid pointing out we barely had the authority to hold a bake sale.

"Whatever. I want her fired," Mandy said. "Like, today." She crossed her arms and stuck her chin up into the air.

"We can't have her fired, either. The school employees all belong to a union. The whole thing is outside of the student government's domain. It's up to the administration." I considered pulling the copy of the employee union agreement out of my file, but I was pretty sure no one was interested in the details of due process. It wasn't exactly a big pro-union crowd. I didn't know why we bothered to have this issue on the agenda at all, except for the fact that everyone wanted to talk about it.

"Really?" Mandy raised one perfectly plucked eyebrow. "If the administration isn't interested in what students think, maybe I should have my parents give them a call."

Mandy's parents have more money than most countries. I was pretty sure they could buy up some small ones—Luxembourg or the Philippines, for example—without even breaking the monthly budget. Her great-grandparents had owned several oil and gas companies and hung out with people like the Vanderbilts. If her parents called the school administration and said jump, people there would start leaping around before even bothering to ask how high.

I looked at the clock. We were going to run out of time. In addition to tackling the safety issue I had hoped to discuss, the council meeting was supposed to be focused on choosing between the two possible themes for our spring formal dance. Any talk of Southern Nights or Old Hollywood had gone out the door when the news about the picture had spread across campus. It was standing room only in the classroom we used for our meetings. No one wanted to miss any hot dirt.

"It totally grosses me out that that dyke took my picture."

Mandy made a face like she had just bitten into month-old cottage cheese.

"Careful," Joel said. As the president of the student council, he was always sure to enforce the "respect and dignity" clause in the student handbook. "Her sexual orientation isn't an issue here."

"God, it's not a gay thing. I have tons of family friends who are gay," Mandy said. "'Dyke' is just a description."

It was classic Mandy to make a distinction between okay gay people (those who design houses or clothing, work in Hollywood, or write for the *New Yorker*) and not okay gay people (women who wear flannel shirts from Walmart.) The real issue wasn't the fact that the security guard might be gay, it was that she had a cheap haircut and unshaven legs, and had made a few thousand dollars selling an unflattering photo of Mandy. Even the haircut, flannel, and legs might have been forgiven if the photo hadn't made Mandy's thighs look a bit chunky.

Joel clapped his hands together to get everyone's attention. "Hailey is right. This issue doesn't fall under student government business." The crowd in the room started to grumble and protest and Joel held up one hand. "That doesn't mean we can't make it our business."

A cheer went up from the group. Joel is a natural politician. I was certain he would be president of the United States someday. He had written to every living former president and asked them for advice on leadership. He kept the letters he got back in a binder in his room. President Clinton had sent him at least four. Not many people can list a President of the United States as a pen pal.

Joel stood so the people at the back could see him. "Privacy and the ability of everyone to feel safe here at Evesham are critical, and are values this government is willing to fight to uphold. This isn't just a boarding school; it's our home away from home. We go to school here. We live here. We need to feel safe here. I motion that the council write a formal letter to the school administration indicating our concerns and demanding that action be taken. All in favor?"

There was a chorus of cheers and whoops from the crowd. Joel looked at me, and I could see the corner of his mouth twitching as he fought off a smile. He knew we could write all the letters we wanted and the school administration would still do whatever they wanted. However, he'd convinced everyone that he was practically Superman standing up for truth, justice, and the American way. Saving the rich and privileged from unflattering photos. I rolled my eyes at him and pressed my mouth together to avoid smiling. If I gave him any encouragement, there was no telling what he would come up with next.

I heard a sound behind me and I turned to see my boyfriend Tristan leaning in the doorway.

Want more funny? Here's a peek at

WHAT WOULD EMMA DO?

by Eileen Cook

God, I've been thinking about our relationship. The way I see it, most people look at you as either (a) a Santa Claus figure they pray to only when they want something, their wishes granted depending on if they are on the naughty or nice list, or (b) a bearded vengeance seeker who gets his immortal jollies from smiting those who annoy him. It occurs to me I've been talking to you my whole life and I don't really know who you are. In fairness, I've always relied on formal prayers, which really haven't given you a chance to get to know me, either. I'm thinking we need a bit more honesty in our relationship—you strike me as the kind to support honesty—so from here on I'm just going to tell you what's on my mind.

We spend a lot of time at Trinity Evangelical Secondary discussing "What would Jesus do?" You have to wonder how the Son of God finds himself in so many ethically questionable situations. I'm guessing he hangs out with a bad crowd.

We've covered how Jesus feels about:

- low-rise jeans (negative)
- underage drinking (although this is the same man who brought us wine transformed from water, we've decided he would just say no)
- gossip (to be avoided—which goes to show he would never make it in Wheaton, where gossip has been perfected to near Olympic levels)

All in all, the Son of God is coming across as a very no-fun kind of guy. I prefer to see him as not so uptight. This puts me in the minority here, where the motto for our church could be "Trinity Evangelical: Sitting in judgment on others since 1849."

At the moment we were supposed to be discussing in great detail, as if this is an issue the president of the United States might need to consult us on, what Jesus would do if he accidentally came across the answers to the math test before the exam. Everyone stared off into space, pondering how our savior might handle this tricky situation.

I left the issue of exam ethics to my capable classmates and went back to trying to get my best friend Joann's attention. I risked a look over my shoulder at her. Mr. Reilly, our religion teacher, has been known to hurl erasers at the heads of students he feels aren't paying attention, so being subtle was key. Joann was either ignoring me or in a catatonic state. I gave a fake cough to draw her attention. Nothing. I coughed again, this time drawing it out as if I might be in the final stages of TB, but not even a glance.

Darci Evers raised one perfectly manicured hand in the air. Darci looks like she jumped out of a spread in *Seventeen* and the teachers always talk about how she makes a great role model, but don't be fooled. She's the kind of person who laughs if you trip in the cafeteria. If your mom forces you to wear the sweater your nearly blind grandmother knit for you, she gives a brittle, thin smile and says, "Nice sweater." Then her posse of friends giggle. In elementary school she dotted the *i* in her name with bubbles and hearts.

"If Jesus saw the test before the exam, he would tell the teacher and ask for a new test, one where he didn't know the answers," Darci said. She paused, her head cocked to the side as if she was getting direct communication from heaven. "Our Lord doesn't like cheaters."

I fought the urge to roll my eyes. The rest of the class all nodded, seemingly relieved to have this conundrum solved and Christ no longer at risk for blowing the hell out of the bell curve. Mr. Reilly smiled. He adores Darci Evers.

"Excellent answer."

I raised my hand. Mr. Reilly's smile withered.

"God is all-knowing, right?" I asked.

"Yes, Emma. He knows everything, what you've done and even what you will do." Mr. Reilly took this moment to look out over the classroom in case anyone had evil or impure thoughts in their hearts.

I looked to see if Joann was following my line of intellectual debate. Joann has never been a huge Darci fan, and I figured it wouldn't hurt to remind her that we had this in common.

"So if God knows everything, won't he know what questions the teacher is going have on the new test too?"

Mr. Reilly's head started to turn red, and I could see the vein in his forehead bulge. For a guy so close to Jesus, he has a lot of repressed rage issues.

"Are you trying to be smart?" Mr. Reilly said.

I hate questions like this. There is no right answer. If

you say you are trying to be smart, you get in trouble for being a wiseass, and if you say you're not, you're admitting to being stupid. It's what they call a lose-lose situation. What would Jesus do if faced with this question? I'm guessing he would go for honesty, but Jesus didn't have to worry about getting lower than a C in class and losing his track eligibility as a result.

"No, sir," I answered.

Mr. Reilly gave a snort and turned back to the board. Darci shot me a look of annoyance and raised her hand again. Joann still wasn't paying any attention to me.

"Mr. Reilly, do you mind if I make an announcement? It's related to student council business," Darci said.

Darci never misses an opportunity to make an announcement. She finds excuses in nearly every class to take center stage. I suspect that if it were up to her as senior class president, she would get to wear a small crown or sash to denote her overall superiority. I'm shocked she doesn't demand that the rest of us scatter palm fronds on the floor in front of her as she walks through the halls.

"As everyone knows, the big spring dance is coming up in just a few weeks, and we still need volunteers to help with the decorations. This year we've selected the theme 'Undersea Adventure.' Please show your school spirit by helping to make this a great event. Even if you haven't been asked to the dance, you could still decorate. We'll be accepting nominations for king and queen for the next two weeks, and the three couples that get the most votes will be announced as the court. The queen and king will be announced at the dance."

"I nominate you," Kimberly said so quickly she must have bumped her nose on the way to kissing Darci's ass.

Darci placed a hand on her heart as if she were overcome by the honor.

"Why, Kimberly, thank you so much! I feel a bit funny about putting myself down on the list, but if you insist." She pulled out her pink gel pen to inscribe her name before she forgot it.

"Why do we even have a king and queen?" I asked.

"We've always had a king and queen of the spring dance. It's tradition," Darci shot back.

"Maybe it's time for a new tradition." As the challenge shot out of my mouth, I couldn't tell who was more surprised, Darci or me. It felt like the air was sucked out of the room for a second as people held their breath, waiting for Darci to whack me back down to size. At least I had Joann's attention now.

"You can't have a new tradition. Then it's not tradition,

it's the opposite; it's new," Darci said, giving me a look, as if shocked that someone of my low intelligence was even allowed in school.

I slunk down in my seat.

"What would Jesus do?" asked Todd.

The entire class turned around to face him. Todd Seaver is the guy in our class who never says anything. There have been rumors that he's an elective mute. Todd has the dubious honor of being from "away," a non-Wheaton native.

"What are you talking about?" Darci asked.

"Would Jesus approve of people setting themselves above others? Sounds like false gods."

"It's not like that at all. Besides, you're Jewish, how would you even know what Jesus would do?"

There was a gasp. It's an unwritten rule that we don't bring up Todd's Jewishness. In a town that is all born-again, his religion is like a deformity, one of those things everyone is painfully aware of and tries to act like they don't notice.

"He was one of the tribe when he started out, you know," Todd said. "I'm thinking he would see the whole king and queen thing as a bunch of false idols, golden calves." He gave Darci a lazy half smile and then looked over at me.

I slunk farther down in my seat, not meeting his eyes. If I went any lower I would slide completely out of the chair and onto the floor. Part of me was glad someone else was standing up to Darci. I just wished the person I was aligned with wasn't the class pariah.

"Interesting point," Mr. Reilly said, tapping his thin fingers on his Bible. He adored Darci, but stamping out fun was his favorite thing in the world.

"It's tradition," said Darci, her voice cracking.

"I think we need to discuss the dance at the next advisory board meeting," Mr. Reilly said as the bell rang.

Darci's mouth opened and shut silently like a fish flopping on a dock. A fish with pink-bubble-gum-scented lip gloss. Everyone got up and moved toward the door. I stood up and grabbed my bag.

Darci bumped into my back. "Way to go, Emma," she hissed, shoving past me.

"Yeah, way to go," Kimberly parroted, following two steps behind her.

Joann walked up next to me, and I gave her a smile.

"My mom already bought me a dress for the dance," she said, crossing her arms. "Why can't you leave some things alone?" She walked away without another word.

Recent events, combined with years of religious study, have clarified for me that at the ripe age of seventeen, I am pretty much already damned to hell. Let's recap:

The Seven Deadly Sins

- Gluttony: I have, on more than one occasion, eaten the entire gut-buster ice-cream sundae at the Dairy Hut that you get for free if you can finish it. What can I say? I run a lot; I get hungry.

- Greed: I have a passion for my running shoe collection that others might reserve for the members of a boy band. It's not just fashion; it's also about function.

- Sloth: Every time my mom sees the state of my room, she is compelled to say, "If you're waiting for the maid to come along, you've got a long wait ahead of you." Then she sighs deeply, like being my mother is her burden in life.

- Wrath: I detest Darci Evers, and if I had the opportunity it is quite likely I would replace her shampoo with Nair.

- Envy: I would give just about anything, including possibly my soul, to run like Sherone Simpson (ranked number one in the world for the hundred meters).

- Pride: I won the state championship last year for hurdles and plan to repeat this year. I've been accepted to Northwestern, and if I can nail down a track scholarship, I've even got a way to pay for it and a way out of town.
- Lust: I kissed my best friend's boyfriend over Christmas break.

Yep, it's pretty much the last one that's going to do me in.

About the Author

E ileen Cook spent most of her teen years wishing she were someone else or somewhere else, which is great training for a writer. When she was unable to find any job postings for world-famous author, she went to Michigan State University and became a counselor so she could at least afford her book-buying habit. But real people have real problems, so she turned to writing because she liked having the ability to control the ending. Which is much harder with humans.

You can read more about Eileen, her books, and the things that strike her as funny at **eileencook.com**. Eileen lives in Vancouver with her husband and dogs, and no longer wishes to be anywhere else.

When the pressures of prep school build up,
cracks can appear in the funniest places.

LEILA SALES

mostly good girls

From Simon Pulse
Published by Simon & Schuster

Love. Heartbreak.
Friendship. Trust.

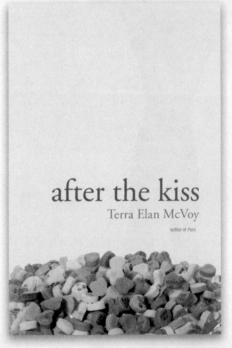

after the kiss

Terra Elan McVoy

author of *Pure*

"I love this book. Like, love it love it.
My heart expanded when I
read it—yours will too."
—Lauren Myracle,
bestselling author of *ttyl* and *ttfn*

From Simon Pulse
Published by Simon & Schuster

Feisty. Flirty. Fun. Fantastic.

one night
that changes everything

LAUREN BARNHOLDT

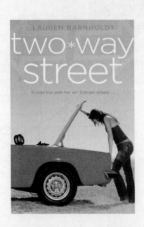